More Praise for *The Un*

"This is a strange, haunting meditation on aloneness and the melancholy of frustrated love, written knowingly about a character bereft of self-knowledge. The language is precise and considered, the mood sustained, the effect at once narrative and poetic. A lovely, elegant debut novel."

—ANDREW SOLOMON, author of *The Noonday Demon*, winner of the National Book Award, and *Far From the Tree*, winner of the National Book Critics Circle Award

"A wonderfully controlled portrait of a contemporary Underground Man—a man who buries his life beneath the normal social interactions of modern-day Manhattan, so that what is inside of him might stay buried too."

—JONATHAN DEE, author of *The Privileges*, a finalist for the Pulitzer Prize

"Pamela Erens's *The Understory* is at once an exquisite portrait of a man driven by forces beyond his control, an homage to Manhattan's secret places, and a deftly braided narrative that keeps the reader hungry to find out what happens next."

—RILLA ASKEW, author of *Fire in Beulah*, winner of the American Book Award

"Mesmerizing . . . a universal human cry for love."

—*ForeWord Magazine*

"An elegant, understated study of physical and psychic dislocations . . . artfully detailed and beautifully rendered."

—*Chicago Tribune*

the Understory

TIN HOUSE BOOKS / Portland, Oregon & Brooklyn, New York

the Understory

a novel

Pamela Erens

Published by Tin House Books, Portland, Oregon, and Brooklyn, New York

Distributed to the trade by Publishers Group West, 1700 Fourth St., Berkeley, CA 94710, www.pgw.com

Library of Congress Cataloging-in-Publication Data has been applied for.

Second U.S. edition, 2014
Printed in the USA
Interior design by Diane Chonette
www.tinhouse.com

for JDR, AER, *and* HER

Character is habit long continued.

—Plutarch

One

Many years ago, in a deli, I found flaky white bits floating in my self-serve coffee; the milk, sitting all day in a bucket of cold water, had turned sour. Since that day I have never drunk my coffee anything but black. Yet I look for those tainted curls every time: I pour, peer inside to reassure myself, then top it off.

Even here I am bound to my habits. I pour, pause, bend to my mug. All at once Joku is standing next to me at the end of the buffet table. He looks down, as if he too suspects that something is wrong with my drink. I move the mug away, toward me, and by the time I have accomplished this I've forgotten my most recent action. Did I already look inside? I think so, but it nags at me that I don't know for sure. The glass coffeepot, suspended above the mug, is beginning to hurt my wrist. Joku is watching me now, and I become even more flustered and uncomfortable. To look twice is not good, not the way things should be, but I decide it is better than failing to look at all. So I glance in, confirm that the surface of the coffee is black and pure, then finish filling the mug and replace the pot on the electric hot plate. Joku moves off, toward the metal trays of kidney beans and homemade bread and peanut butter.

Normally his staring wouldn't rattle me so much. I have grown used to it. He watches me in the dining hall, during chores, as we file into the meditation hall for *zazen*. He is so open about it, does not spy or hide. His head turns as we pass in the hallways. Without a doubt the abbot has asked him to keep tabs on me. For what if I am mentally unbalanced, a troublemaker? But today was different. Today Joku came so close that he nearly touched me.

He was the first person I met here, with the exception of the secretary. I was dirty from the night in the park and the day on the bus, and the red itchy blossoms on my neck and arms tormented me. Warily the secretary invited me in out of the snow, but I stayed under the eaves next to the large oak door with its brass doorknob while she ran to see what was to be done about me. It was only on the last leg of the trip that the snow had begun. When I'd left Manhattan it had been spring, but now, three hundred miles north, it was winter again, the land knocked back into dormancy. The sun was setting and I watched the spruce and firs below the hill sink into darkness. Then a small man in a dark robe came to the entrance. He had a broad, intelligent face and wire-rimmed glasses. I guessed him to be ten years older than I was, around fifty. "Mr. Ronan?" he asked. "My name is Joku." He flung his hand toward the open door, indicating that I had been received, admitted. His gesture was too big; the back of his hand hit the door, made a leaden thud.

He led me through the simple corridors—unsanded beams, white plaster, flowers set in a wall alcove. I pictured Patrick passing through these hallways and wanted to reach out to touch the walls that he might have touched, but we were moving quickly and I did not want to call attention to myself. We arrived at a small office and the monk introduced me to the abbot, a tall man with a long, elegant head who sat at a desk bare of papers. The monk withdrew to the side of the room but could not seem to make himself unobtrusive. He shuffled, coughed, knocked over something on a table.

"Are you interested in our practice?" asked the abbot, resting his arms upon his desk. I had not expected him to look and sound so perfectly American. His voice had a Yankee timbre, the elegant head a Yankee frigidity. I answered that I didn't know. I repeated what I had said to the secretary, that I had no home, no place to stay. I waited to be asked for more details. But the abbot only handed me a folded piece of paper and told the monk to find me a bed. And so I was taken to a room with four bunk beds and given a pillow and a small rough towel. Looking at the beds, I could already feel the nearness of the bodies that would lie in them tonight. Snow drizzled steadily outside the window. The fire under my skin brought water to my eyes and

I slapped heavily at my arms, then pushed up my sleeve to show the monk that there was a reason, that it wasn't craziness. His eyes widened. "What is it?" he asked.

"Nothing contagious," I assured him. "An allergic reaction."

"I will find something for you," he told me.

The room was empty and quiet; the whole building was quiet. I looked at the paper the abbot had given me. It spelled out the abbey's policy on nonpaying visitors. Short-term residencies would be permitted in exchange for twenty hours of labor a week. A list followed; I was to check off any areas in which I had special skill. *Cooking. Computers. Communications. Gardening.* And so on. Across the list I scrawled the word *none.* Then I erased that—better to appear useful—and put a check mark next to *Gardening.*

The monk came back with a crumpled tube. "*Tch, tch,*" he clucked as I patted the ointment on. A strange, sorrowful little noise. I sighed as the cool salve penetrated the skin.

"We rise at four," said the monk. "Just follow the others."

"My name is Gorse, actually."

"Pardon me?" He stopped at the door.

"I said Ronan but that's not correct. My name is Gorse, Jack Gorse."

"Mr. Gorse, then. Pleased to meet you."

I was afraid he would hold out his hand. The fleshiness of a handshake has always repelled me, hands slickly moist or hot like a furnace. But he only bowed, Buddhist-style, his thick palms pressed together. He told me to make myself comfortable, and added that the others would be back in half an hour. The lights would be turned out at nine.

It felt good to have a bed. I fell asleep before the others returned.

Two

In Chinatown the late-November air smelled of raw fish, and the sidewalk was full of orange rinds and trampled paper. I'd entered the neighborhood via the Bowery, right on schedule. Night was falling and men and women hurried by on their way home, carrying bulging scarlet plastic bags filled with fruit and fish and vegetables. As I passed yet another greengrocer's I caught sight of two stout men rooting through a sidewalk bin stacked high with yellow squash, and so I stopped a few feet away. I always stop if I think I see a pair of twins, even if it risks disrupting my schedule. Usually, of course, it's a false alarm. The light over the bins was dim, so I could not see the men's features clearly. I moved to a different part of the sidewalk, but it was even harder to see from there. Still, I had a feeling I was right. The men's broad foreheads and wide noses, moving in and out of the shadows, seemed cut from the same mold. I rummaged around in a bin of garlic, pretending to pick out the best specimens. After a few minutes one of the men made an impatient comment and the other man followed him out.

I watched them for as long as I could, until they disappeared, two shrinking forms, around a corner. Now I would never know for sure. Let me explain. I hunt for twins. Not your run-of-the-mill fraternals, your IVF side effects, but identicals only, life's natural aberrations. Nothing so far but Nature can make these mirror images, her rare gift of likeness in a world of infinite variety. Successful sightings are very unusual, but I wake up each morning with a sense of expectation, knowing that *unusual* does not mean *impossible*, armed with the statistic that the incidence of natural-born identicals is roughly three in a thousand. In a city like Manhattan, where a man with a habit of walking may pass thousands of people each day, the unusual must occasionally come to pass. And so it does. In the summer I came across two sisters leaving the main post office on Eighth Avenue wearing identical faces and identical postal uniforms. A few months before that it was two brothers with identical toupees feeding the pigeons in Union Square. During the long stretches between sightings I kept my spirits up by convincing myself I saw twins separated from their doubles. *There*, I would tell myself, spotting a man listing slightly to one side, as if leaning his weight on another person, or a woman constantly glancing next to her, perhaps checking for her invisible other: *a shard, a half.*

I was disappointed that the two men had walked off before I had been able to get a really good look. I never follow people. It would embarrass me, and besides, it would throw off my schedule. I brushed some papery garlic skin from my jacket sleeve and went on my way, completing my daily walk from the Upper West Side to the Brooklyn Bridge. The last stretch of streets before the bridge always made me gloomy. After Canal Street Chinatown dissolves into the municipal district, with its ugly horizontal architecture, its clouds of dirty pigeons, its stream of distressed visitors. Lawyers leap out of taxis, thousands of lawyers on their way to family court, divorce court, housing court, criminal court. The buildings bear big block letters: POLICE, PROBATION, DETENTION. I always felt uneasy passing through. But soon, blessedly, I would be at the bridge, where my evening ended with a climb to the top of the wooden pedestrian walkway. There, a hundred feet above the water, neither in Manhattan nor in Brooklyn but somewhere between, I would glimpse on my right the Statue of Liberty, on my left the echo of the Manhattan Bridge. Ahead of me was the Brooklyn tower, with its caisson sunk deep into Brooklyn bedrock and its cables that seemed to invite you to pull yourself hand over hand along them until you got across. But I never did go across. I had lived my entire life in Manhattan and had never been to Brooklyn. There had never been any reason to go. Suspended between the two banks, I would breathe in the night air and watch the boats with their night lights move past the harbor. Then

I would go back down the way I had come and head toward the subway. I had done this nearly every evening for more than fourteen years.

My subway was the C train stopping at 6:27 at the Broadway-Nassau station. Most New Yorkers do not realize that the subways run on a precise schedule. They might not care about catching a 5:13 or a 6:27; they come to their station and wait and before long a train arrives. But I liked, whenever possible, to be on one particular train. I got onto the third car, as usual. The man with the square glasses and very flat briefcase was sitting in his favorite seat under the subway map opposite the doors. The short-haired woman with the frown was at the other end of the same row of seats. Long ago I had decided that this woman made this trip uptown every few nights to see a lover, a man who met with her before going home to his family for the evening. The man meant more to her than she meant to him. The pinched and anxious lines between the woman's eyes were what made me think so; also, she carried nothing with her except a small beige purse with a twisted silk rope for a strap. A small paperback always peeked out of the top of the purse. Sometimes the man under the map caught my eye and nodded. The woman always behaved as if she had never seen me before.

The train rocked, warm and not too crowded as yet. There were twenty-one minutes, assuming no unexpected delays, before I would arrive at my stop. I began to wonder whether Mrs. Fiore would be waiting for me on the landing, insisting on a talk. We had been neighbors for nearly fifteen years, and she had known my uncle before me, but we had hardly exchanged a word until the previous winter, when Paul Giglio had purchased our Upper West Side brownstone from Morris Skill, our longtime landlord. Skill lived in El Paso, Texas, and never set foot in the place: the perfect landlord, as far as I was concerned. The first thing Giglio had done was to offer Mrs. Fiore and me and Mr. Flax on the fourth floor and the Porters in the garden duplex ten thousand dollars each to move. He made no secret of his plans to renovate the four existing floor-throughs and bring them up to market rate. When none of us agreed to the ten thousand dollars, Giglio shut off the heat. That took care of Mr. Flax, who contracted pneumonia, and the Porters, who were expecting a baby. Mrs. Fiore began to wait for me in the hallways. She had no one else to pester; even the super was gone, fired by Giglio some months before. What would it be this time? A request to borrow some butter? A demand that I recalculate her grocery bill? Mrs. Fiore suspected cheating among the cashiers at Key Food. As I approached my building, gauging how quickly I might be able to get past her, I saw the outer door swing open and a tall man rush out, his head down. I steeled myself to stop him and demand what his business was, but when I stepped into his path his head snapped up and I saw his frightened face. We were both startled at having nearly knocked into each other. He searched my own face for a moment, then seemed to recover himself.

"I'm sorry," he said. "Do you live here?"

I nodded.

"Tell your neighbor that I'm just the architect," he said. "Mr. Giglio sent me." He dipped a hand into his pocket and drew out a card. I had a moment to look at him now. He had a long face, high cheekbones, pale eyes, and a long, shapeless coat. He was twenty-seven or twenty-eight, perhaps. Something else struck me about him, and in a moment I knew what it was: he had that odd, unverifiable aura of being a twin. There seemed to be someone absent standing next to him, a kink of loneliness in his posture. I took the card from him. It bore a name, Patrick Allegra, along with the name of an architectural firm in the West Twenties.

"I need to take some pictures," he said. He raised a camera hanging by a strap over his shoulder, by way of proof. "I think I alarmed your neighbor, Mrs., um . . ."

"Fiore," I said. "You're here to look at the vacated apartments?"

It had been hours since I had spoken to anyone, and my voice was raspy. I cleared my throat.

His eyes slid away. "I'm here to look at all of the apartments," he said.

"I still happen to live in mine," I told him.

"Yes, I know. It's what Mr. Giglio has asked me to do."

I wondered how much Giglio had told him about me. *Illegal tenant, pays only two hundred and ten dollars a month, unemployed, bit of a crank.* The architect picked at his collar with palpable unease. "I would be happy to work around

your schedule," he said. "Just let me know a time that's convenient for you."

In my schedule there is no time for interruptions, devia-
tions. But I did not want to get into this with him. "Come
back another time," I told him, pushing open the door. I
kicked some delivery menus and a crumpled paper bag out
of my way and opened my mailbox, drew out a thin pile of
mail. As I walked up the steps I could feel Mrs. Fiore's presence above me, hovering.

"Jack? Is that you?"

"Yes," I answered. Mrs. Fiore had many times urged me
to call her Frances, but that felt uncomfortably familiar in
my mouth. When I called her Mrs. Fiore, however, I got a
lecture, and so, on the occasions when we spoke, I avoided
using any name at all.

She came down the steps as quickly as her legs allowed.
First I glimpsed her slippers cut open at the front to give air
to her swollen toes, then her quilted housecoat, and finally
her long reddish braid. Sometimes, when she was not well,
she would let her hair go loose, and then it fell past her hips:
astonishingly thick, strong, rust-colored hair that forced
me to imagine younger years and children begging for the
privilege of braiding it. She'd been a mother of seven, and in
the tales she told me (buttonholing me on the stairs when
I wanted to go inside and read, until I shook with impatience) she was forever a woman stirring a pot with a baby
draped over her shoulder and another child tugging on her
skirt. In the corners of this picture little boys wrestled, girls

smeared lipstick on their dolls, puppies yipped and peed on the carpets. Being with Mrs. Fiore was enough to make me feel crowded, that I had not enough room on the stair.

Today she was agitated, breathing rapidly. "Thank God," she panted, one hand on the quilted spot over her heart. "I heard the door downstairs and I came out, thinking it was you. But it wasn't. So I screamed, but he kept coming up the stairs, talking and coming."

"It was just the architect," I told her. I showed her the card he had given me.

She frowned, bit her lip. "Yes, but—," she said, and with a bent finger she tapped on my door.

Thumbtacked over the peephole was a sheet of paper with the words NOTICE OF TERMINATION typed at the top. I had expected a seal, fancy script, a bit of pomp. I took down the paper and read it through quickly. It stated that I, John Frederick Ronan Gorse, was illegally occupying premises rented to John Frederick Ronan, and that I was expected to remove myself within ten days.

"What are you going to do?" Mrs. Fiore asked. Mrs. Fiore always had questions. Usually they were the same ones, over and over. *You used to be a lawyer, didn't you? Could Mr. Giglio evict me? Could he raise my rent?* I always told her that the matter was out of our hands, that we would just have to wait and see what Giglio would do. I'd remind her that she'd been a legal tenant for more than thirty years. I'd stress the word *legal* so that she would get the point: I was the one who had something to worry about.

Yes, but, she would say, always, *Yes, but,* and finally it had dawned on me: as afraid as she was of being thrown out, she was even more afraid of being left alone. Alone in the building with all the worries a seventy-eight-year-old woman can conjure up: thieves, rapists, murderers. She paid only three hundred dollars a month in rent; how could she leave? But if I were evicted, how could she stay? When she asked, *What are you going to do?* what she really wanted to know was, *What will I do if you leave?*

"I don't know," I said.

She clutched her robe at the neck and said she didn't want the architect coming into her place.

I took out my keys.

Her hand reached out and grabbed my arm. I flinched. Although she often stood too close to me, she had never touched me before. I could smell her smell, a mixture of soap and something deeper, unwashable.

"My son-in-law is worse," she said.

I grunted to make her think I was listening. But really I was paying attention to my breathing, in and out, so as to be less aware of her fingers like bands around my arm.

"One-bedroom apartment," I heard her say. "Sharon can't possibly take me in." I had heard this story many times before: the daughter in Neptune, New Jersey, the son-in-law with multiple sclerosis, the tiny apartment, the impossibility of going to live with them. The other children lived much farther away, in Texas, Arizona, Germany.

"Yes," I muttered.

"I know you'll know just what to do."

She released her grip and I escaped into my apartment.

I threw my coat onto the sofa and the notice on top of it, then flipped through my mail. There were three solicitations and one bill, all addressed to Mr. Ronan. I tossed the solicitations unopened into the wastepaper basket. The bill was from the electric company, and the figure seemed high. I squinted at the small print and saw that the rates had gone up. One envelope remained, this one addressed to John F.R. Gorse. I opened it to find the check for five hundred dollars that always arrived around this time of the month. In the lower right-hand corner was the spidery signature of my parents' executor. Always that handwriting conjured up for me the visit to his office after my parents' death so many years ago, the pad he pushed across the table after scribbling some figures on it, too embarrassed, apparently, to say the numbers aloud.

"Your parents lived a little too well," he'd said with an uneasy smile. "And they had their pet charities." I stared at the pad: a five followed by two zeros. That was what my inheritance came to, five hundred dollars a month. And the principal? I asked him. The executor fidgeted. "After your death," he said, "it will go to Actors' Equity. I'm afraid that you won't be able to touch it."

I put the check aside and thought of the young man with the long face and pale eyes who wanted to take some pictures. I tried to remember the last time that anyone other than me had stood in these rooms. It must have been two

years ago in the spring, when a plumber replaced a cor-
roded faucet. Morris Skill never fixed anything; that was
understood. I accepted that without protest, since at one
time or another Skill must have figured out that I was illegal and yet he'd always left me alone. I'd stood next to the
plumber and noted the things he touched, and after he left
I wiped off everything with a damp rag.

My book was lying on the table next to the sofa. All day
I had looked forward to returning to it, but it no longer
held any interest for me. Instead I did what I always did
when I was troubled or distracted: I stood at my bookshelves and waited for the right book to reveal itself. The
shelves, of thick oak, took up an entire wall and had been
installed by my uncle. The bottom shelves were filled with
the books he himself had left behind: accounts of military campaigns, political theory going back to Plato, and
a generous collection of anarchist writings. On the shelves
above were books I'd taken from my parents' townhouse
when I sold it to pay off their debts: scripts of the plays
my mother had appeared in; biographies and memoirs
of famous stage actors and actresses, many of whom had
worked with her and had visited our cavernous apartment
on East Sixty-Third. At the very top were the books I'd
bought when I still had money to buy books, a mishmash
of philosophy, law, ancient literature, history, chemistry,
and botany. At the end of one row was a scrapbook that
I had put together when I was thirteen years old and that
contained only three items—an enormous maple leaf, a

slip of paper with the words *jewel beetle* written on it, and the soaked-off label of a can of Campbell's tomato soup.

I could hear Mrs. Fiore shuffling about upstairs, a clatter of dishes in her kitchen, the television going on. Either she did not sleep well or she had a tendency to doze off while watching, because I sometimes woke in the middle of the night to hear the grumble of TV laughter. The air in the apartment smelled metallic tonight, a sign of the first deepening of fall into winter. I put on a sweater and looked through the open cabinet of LPs next to the stereo. My uncle had collected hundreds of recordings: a bit of jazz, some classical, lots of opera. Studying them one by one soothed me. I put on Tchaikovsky's Trio in A Minor and waited for the throat-clearing static of the needle finding its groove. Then came the low notes of the piano, followed immediately by the entrance of the melancholy cello and the echo of the violin. I listened with my eyes closed, my feet up on the coffee table, to the fluid but insistent repetitions. I thought of my uncle, home at night after work, reclining very likely in this same position on this same sofa, listening to this same trio, twenty or thirty or forty years ago. I could even picture my mother beside him, in those early days when she'd first come to New York to live with him, following the trail he'd blazed. They were Quakers, fallen away. Plain people, attracted by the big city. I could see her twisting her handkerchief, confessing, *I don't love God as much as I love Portia or Viola or Blanche DuBois. I don't love God as much as I love makeup and costumes. God wants me to be plain and I can't be plain.* And my uncle would have answered, *That's all right, Grace. God gave up on me a long time ago.*

I rose to make myself a sandwich. My book from the night before still waited: Schopenhauer, *The World as Will and Representation.* I picked it up and put it down again. I returned to the bookcase and pulled down one book after another. Some nights it took me an hour or more before I could find the right book, the one that would make me forget anything I might be feeling, the day's complications and demands. This would be one of those evenings. My mind kept straying to Mrs. Fiore's crooked finger tapping my door, the architect's long face. I walked to the window to watch the hurrying bodies below. I did not want the architect to come into my rooms. Those rooms were arranged in a very particular way and had been for a long time. When I'd moved in I had taken care not to change by even a few inches the position of my uncle's sofa and chairs, or of any of his other things. Perhaps this was a way to complete my impersonation of him. But in any case, that arrangement felt at first familiar and comforting, and then necessary. This Patrick Allegra would surely move something, alter something, and I would be able to feel the difference. Even if I were to put things back in order later on, it would not be the same: the vibration of change would remain. I remained at the window thinking thoughts like these until it occurred to me that the radiator against my knees was completely cold. I reached down and touched it, just to be sure. It was something I ought to have anticipated.

I made plenty of noise as I took the stairs into the basement, in order to scare off the rats. There were no lights down here—Giglio kept removing the bulbs and I had grown tired of replacing them—but with my flashlight I found the furnace. I ducked down next to it, looking for the dial. The previous winter, Giglio and I had engaged for several months in an elaborate game of cat and mouse. He turned off the heat; I turned it back on. No sooner had the rooms warmed up than Giglio would return, often late at night, so that I would awaken the next morning huddled against the cold.

The dial, I saw, had been padlocked. It sat in a small cage with narrow openings too small to poke a finger through. Momentarily I was impressed with Giglio's foresight. I worked at the lock with a paper clip I found in my pocket, then searched around for something more effective. In a corner full of dirt and laundry lint I found a hammer with a metal head. I hit the lock repeatedly, to no effect. Then I hit the cage. I hit it until pain pulsed in my wrist and shoulder. The bars bent but would not break. I threw the hammer to the floor, panting, and stared at the furnace, wishing for another idea. The basement smelled of rat droppings and damp Sheetrock and dust.

It's all right, I thought, as I returned to my apartment. I know what to do. From a drawer I removed last winter's sleeping outfit: an old pair of corduroys, a turtleneck, and a wool sweater. I remembered the other things that would follow now: the painful morning hopping and stamping to get the blood flowing back into my feet, the cups of scalding coffee, the evenings pressed up against the kitchen oven. I told myself, as I'd told myself the previous year, that my will was stronger than Giglio's, that I would outlast him.

Three

Night is the worst time. After the long regimentation of the day, the enforced silences, the men want to talk. At first it doesn't matter what about: TV, movies, travel, jobs. I lie on my side on my mattress as the words pool around me, reciting to myself the botanical classifications for peach, cherry, apple. *Magnoliophyta, Magnoliopsida, Rosales, Rosaceae* . . . I smell the smell of other bodies: stale skin, flatulence, cologne. I long to open the windows and let the fresh air sweep the smells away, sweep the bodies away, too. Gradually one man drops out of the conversation, then another. Soon there will be only two men left speaking. And now these two—they are not the same two every night—will drop their voices, speak in an intimate murmur. Perhaps they are only gossiping about one of the monks. Perhaps they are complaining about the food. But no, there is a reticence that lets me know that they are trying, clumsily, to reach each other. I crush my pillow against my ears and think of an article I once read in a science magazine. Ultrasound, the author wrote, shows that many pregnancies start out as twin pregnancies. Long before quickening, either the twins merge or one is absorbed by the placenta. Up to fifteen percent of us might actually be the surviving half of a twin pair. I imagine that I am a conjoined creature, two souls wrapped into one, and after a while this thought lulls me to sleep.

We wake at four to the sound of a stick being struck against the door and shuffle to the meditation hall for an hour of morning *zazen*. The abbot sits on a small platform in front of the altar. Behind him narrow windows with iron grillwork show pictures of darkness. I fold my legs, imagining that Patrick once sat on this very buckwheat cushion, once bowed his head and tried like me to bear the loneliness of wakefulness before sunrise. I am sure that I feel his presence here, sure that he preceded me.

Follow your breath, they instruct us, *hear and feel yourself breathe in and breathe out, count these breaths from one to ten and then begin again. Clear your mind of all thought; if any thought arises let it drop like a pebble down a well.* But when the thoughts come I find myself unwilling to shed them so easily. I have no family, no home, no friend, no books. Surely they can leave me my thoughts. Surreptitiously I turn my head to look at the still, obedient bodies around me. Out of the corner of my vision I perceive the monitor with his big stick walking my way and I shrink back into myself, glue my gaze to the floor. I hold

my breath. He passes and I am free. I go back to my thinking. I trace the structure of a sugar molecule, recall passages
in favorite books. I walk through the rooms and hallways
of my childhood home, touching the expensive wallpaper,
the Chinese porcelains, the Rothkos and de Koonings. How
much longer will I be allowed to stay at the abbey? I have a
bank account in Manhattan that holds nearly two thousand
dollars. But it is much too risky to write for the money. My
stomach growls.

At breakfast Joku tries to get my attention. I bend over
my scrambled eggs, pretending I don't see, but he puts his
tray next to mine and begins a conversation. He reminds
me of the form I filled out, the one where I claimed to be
some sort of gardener. He is asking me if I know anything
about bonsai. I say, yes, I do, though I don't think it wise
to add that what I know comes only from books. Joku explains, at some length, that the monastery has a large collection of bonsai and that they have been doing poorly ever
since the monk who used to take care of them left. No one
since then seems to have the knack. I keep nodding intel-
ligently as he speaks, to imply that I feel that this is a great
shame and that I have just the sort of expertise that will save
the day. And although I've said almost nothing during our
conversation, Joku seems pleased and tells me that he will
bring me over to the bonsai shed as soon as possible.

Four

I woke on the living room couch with my book in my hand, the architect's business card stuck in the back pages. The sun was just rising and my toes and fingers were numb. I removed the card from the book and read the words on it again. In the night I had had an idea. If Giglio could play games with locks, so could I. There was a locksmith's a couple of blocks away, on Columbus, but of course it would not be open at this hour. I would go to the park as usual, only cutting my visit a bit short, and in that way could make a brief stop at the locksmith's on my way to Carl's. It would be an expense, to be sure, but it would hardly disrupt my schedule at all. I rubbed the blood back into my hands and splashed water on my face, pushed a book into my overcoat pocket. Then I walked to the corner and crossed the street into Central Park.

In the early morning the park is a great canvas speckled with dog walkers and briefcased workers crossing over to

Midtown. As always, I watched these with the relieved sense
that we would soon be parting ways. Walking warmed me,
and the farther I got from the city streets, the freer I felt.
The day was overcast and windy and I lifted my collar as
I moved briskly in the direction of the lake, watching the
tops of the buildings slowly disappear behind the screen of
trees. By the time I reached the Ramble, nearly the exact
center of the park, I was aware only of my breathing and of
the wind against my face.

The Ramble is the jewel of the park, its secret heart. Frederick Law Olmsted and Calvert Vaux, the park's designers,
created it, I like to think, as a reward for those of us who have
the cunning and patience to uncover it. There are people
who bike in the park, picnic here, walk daily to work, and yet
never find the Ramble. You have to know where to turn off
the main path, and you have to be willing to lose your sense
of direction in this landscape where no exit can be seen on
any side. The paths turn, and every few steps a new arrangement of stone and brush appears and makes you forget the
one you have just passed through and might not easily find
again. The birdwatchers know the Ramble—the birding is
excellent here—and so do the homosexuals. They come here
to meet those they might not meet anywhere else, to tryst in
a place that is somehow both private and exposed.

Entering the Ramble each morning I entered, you might
say, my variety. My daily schedule was fixed: I rose at
daybreak, walked to the park, spent some hours at Carl's
bookstore, had my lunch, walked downtown, climbed the

bridge. It was the park that put the day into a living balance. I knew each turn of the paths and each significant feature, yet never knew exactly what I would find here. The plants blossomed, got uprooted or trampled, reseeded themselves, swiveled toward the sun, bent with the wind. Insects and small animals left their marks. Each day I noticed some living thing or living trace I had missed all the many days before. I liked to imagine what the Ramble looked like when Olmsted and Vaux first created the park: a wild garden of daffodils, tulips, French roses, rhododendrons, Solomon's seal, fox grape, hazelnut, Carolina allspice, and more, a landscape of hills and valleys in which native and exotic trees grew side by side. Since then billions of footfalls had flattened the land and stripped it of some of its most precious features. But I like bare as well as lush, probably better. What speaks to me most is close to the ground: the shrubs and vines, rather than the great elms, oaks, and maples. The understory, as botanists call it. In the decades after the war, when the city turned its back on the park—firing the groundskeepers, ceding greater and greater swaths of land to the muggers and drug dealers—it was not the big trees that began to disappear; it was the shrubs: the witch hazel and jetbead, black haw and sweet pepperbush. The park became like the city: skyscrapers, no texture. And that meant it was dying. The things that live at ground level are what hold the earth fast, buffering the grander plants from flooding, salt, and erosion. Central Park was built on rocky, inhospitable land, and its secret is the shallowness of its soil, its only tenuous ability to sustain life. It is the shrubs that allow the park to survive.

My first stop this morning was to check on a witch-hazel bush that had been vandalized earlier in the fall. I'd found the crime weapon, a broken Bass Ale bottle, lying next to a heap of sawed-off branches. The dismembering had taken some work, given the crudeness of the tool: someone had been very angry, very persistent. A spurned lover? Someone just fired from a job? One of the mentally ill men who circled the park in their baggy pants and unlaced sneakers?

The branches had scarred over nicely, but it was impossible to be sure of this plant until the spring. Soon it would be dormant, healing itself, and if all went well new growth would push forth come April and the spidery yellow blossoms would appear again when the weather cooled. I put my hand to the ground. It was still moist, but the soil was hardening and becoming denser in preparation for the winter. I stroked the trunk of a spindly sassafras, its smooth green pith showing through in places where the wind had scoured off the fragile bark. I cradled one of its last leaves in the palm of my hand. If you blindfolded me I could tell you the name of almost any plant, some by touch, some by smell, different in each season. In the spring and summer I watched my plants flower, but it was, perhaps, in winter that I loved them best, when their skeletons were exposed. Then I felt they had more to say to me, were not simply dressing themselves for the crowds. Stripped of their leaves, their identities showed forth stark, essential.

After a while I made my way to a boulder with a smooth flat top and sat looking out over the cloudy greenish water of a small pond. I drew out the eviction notice and flattened it over my knee. One thing was clear: I was not going to pack up and leave because of a notice on a letterhead. Removing me from the apartment ought to require more of Giglio's time and energy than that. I enjoyed thinking of the trouble my changing the locks would put him to. As for the eviction notice, this evening I would do some research at my old law school library. I very much disliked altering my schedule but the reason was pressing enough.

Once again I pulled out the architect's card. *Patrick Allegra*. His name was appealingly musical. Wasn't *alegre* the Spanish word for *merry*? A sympathetic face, too. I wished that a man employed by Giglio would be easier to despise. I stood up and began to make my way out of the park toward the Upper West Side. I reached the locksmith's shortly after it opened and spoke to the owner, who was the only person there, telling him I needed my lock changed as soon as possible. He said that his associate would be in at any moment and he would meet me at the apartment then; what was the address? That had not been my plan; I had meant to leave a copy of the key to the downstairs door and be on my way. But the man refused to take the key and insisted that he would be over directly. I set off for the apartment.

My block looked odd at this unfamiliar hour, lit by a different angle of light, full of unfamiliar inhabitants. A teen-aged boy and girl who ought to have been in school walked toward me, arm in arm. I was impatient for the locksmith to arrive so that I could take my leave. As I entered the building I heard footsteps heading down the stairs, and I swore silently.

As on the previous night, the architect noticed me only at the last minute. We came face-to-face on my landing. He was humming to himself, something melancholy and a bit off-key, and he stopped, embarrassed. In the daylight I could see the blond hair, straight and lank, that fell to his shoulders. Today he wore jeans and a dark collarless shirt. Around one wrist was a bracelet of brown beads. He smiled and said he had been to the apartments upstairs and was just now about to stop in mine; he was sorry for the imposition. I found myself unlocking my door and letting him in.

He entered, swiveling his head this way and that. I saw him take in the worn tan carpet, the sagging toffee-colored sofa, the antiquated stereo with its outsized speakers. The architect removed his bag—a knapsack, not a briefcase—and leaned it with excessive care against the sofa. Then, excusing himself once again for disturbing me, he walked about the room with his notebook. I retreated to the kitchen to make a cup of coffee, and as I brought it into the living room the buzzer rang. I walked downstairs and told the puzzled locksmith that I had changed my mind, my lock did not need changing after all. I pressed a ten-dollar bill into his hand and went back to the apartment.

With my coffee I sat in the living room, pretending to read but really spying on my visitor, keeping track of anything he might displace. At first he turned toward me every couple of minutes in the hope, apparently, that my attention had wandered. But gradually he began to forget me. He took some pictures, measured the window sashes, the radiator covers. Every time he measured something he would place his hand on it briefly, as if taking its temperature. At first I flinched; then I began to grow used to it. His tape measure made a sound like shaken foil. The more oblivious he became, the more he touched things. He lifted the window drapes, ran his hand slowly over the chairs and along the walls. He began to hum sadly again. I grew uneasy watching him, half expecting that soon he would crouch down and caress the dirty carpet. When he moved in the direction of my bedroom I leaped up in alarm. He noticed me then and spread his palm against the wall.

"This building has lovely bones," he said softly. Again I noticed his pale eyes and almost invisible lashes. "It's a nice old building," he continued. "Sometimes, when you do the demolition, you find real beauties inside. Antique tile. Marble fireplaces." He knocked on the boards sealing up my own fireplace. "It's a scandal that these brownstones were ever allowed to deteriorate like this."

Suddenly he flushed and began to put his camera back into its case. "I didn't mean to say that this apartment is slated for demolition," he said.

"Didn't you?" I asked.

He looped the camera strap over his shoulder and looked at me. "Mr. Giglio told me you've been living here illegally. Is it true?"

"Yes," I answered. I looked around, as if the old stereo and age-worn sofa might speak for me, offer defenses. It seemed to me as if I had only just moved in, as if just the other day an aunt I'd never met had phoned me from Fishertown, Pennsylvania, to tell me that my uncle had passed away. "I was afraid you wouldn't know," she'd said. And I hadn't known; there had been no one to tell me. I hadn't been in touch with my uncle for some years. My aunt began to sob: first it was my mother, she said, now Fred; she was the only one left.

That was when I'd come up with my plan. I'd told my aunt that it was a long trip for her, especially in the state she was in, and that I would be glad to go to the apartment and pack up her brother's things for her. She thanked me, over and over, said I was a good nephew, a fine son; she wished my mother had not been such a stranger. When I got to my uncle's place, carrying one large suitcase, there was little work for me to do. The apartment had all the dusty asceticism I remembered from my childhood. There seemed to be only one of everything: one overcoat, one pot, one wooden spoon. I spent an afternoon boxing up the clothing—too small for me—and taking it to the post office. Everything else I kept, including the bedding and the kitchen items. I wrote my aunt that I had donated these to Goodwill. I slept that night on the sheets my uncle had spent his last night on and felt that in this rather ghoulish way I was earning my right to be there, to inhabit his place.

"I've lived here for fifteen years," I told the architect.

He nodded, dropping his gaze. He seemed easily embarrassed, alternately assertive and retreating. Then, abruptly,
he looked up and thrust out his hand, saying he would be
out of my way now.

I took a step back. The architect dropped his arm, as if
he had expected no better. "Where will you go?" he asked.

My heart skipped a beat. Where would I go? Yes, where?
He was looking down at me, still close enough to resume
that aborted handshake, with what looked like genuine con-
cern. Had he pegged me right off as someone who might,
in fact, have no place to go? I struggled to think of a digni-
fied answer. But just then I recognized Mrs. Fiore's clumsy
footsteps in the stairwell, and we both heard her sharp, annoyed "Oh!" and the sound of something hitting the floor.
We hurried out to the landing. A torn bag of groceries lay
on the floor; Mrs. Fiore bent over it, trying to right a half
gallon of milk. When she saw us she raised herself stiffly.
"Don't worry, Frances," said the architect, coming to her.
"Just take it easy."

Frances, I thought. *I seem to have missed something.*
As the architect helped Mrs. Fiore to her feet I began to
retrieve the cans that had rolled into the corner, setting
them in an orderly row. Then I rearranged the row, placing
the small cans at one end and the larger ones at the other.
Gradually I became aware that the others were waiting for
something else from me. Finally the architect asked me if
I had another shopping bag. I said I did and went to my
kitchen to get it.

When I returned he was telling Mrs. Fiore about an herb treatment that might relieve the pains in her legs. She nodded eagerly. They seemed to be continuing a conversation they'd started earlier. "The ingredients are a little hard to find," he said. "I'll bring them over for you. Try it for a few days and then let me know." The architect and I loaded the fallen groceries into the fresh bag.

"Thank you," said Mrs. Fiore—to the architect, not to me. I was surprised to hear her voice quaver. "You're a good man," she said. She shot a look at me, as if to underscore my shortcomings by comparison. The architect took the bag in one hand and gently cupped Mrs. Fiore's shoulder with the other, waiting for her to start up the steps. He walked at a creeping pace, never getting ahead of her. *Yes, where will I go?* I wondered.

It was nearly noon by the time I arrived at Egret Books, a used bookstore on Columbus Avenue in the upper Sixties. Egret had a punched-tin ceiling and a string of bells looped over the door to alert Carl when a customer came in, although he was almost always at the large desk at the front, going through paperwork. Egret was small and much of its stock consisted of predictable secondhand leftovers: novels by Howard Fast and James Gould Cozzens, "treasuries" of humor from the 1940s, books about fishing and dogs. There were other, better-stocked stores I sometimes visited, but Egret was the only one at which I was a regular. I felt comfortable there. White-haired, hunching Carl never bothered me with conversation or seemed to mind that I did not buy anything. He hardly seemed to register that I was there.

Carl held up his palm in greeting, without lifting his eyes from his papers. "Hello, Ronan," he said. I moved past him into the mouth of the store. For some reason I always thought of Carl as Charon, the silent old man who ferried souls into the Land of the Dead. Perhaps it was the dim lighting and labyrinth-like layout of Egret. Or perhaps it was the way my mind circled deeper and deeper the longer I spent at the shelves, until it reached an almost still point: not the frozenness of eternal torment but the stasis of perfect absorption.

First, however, there was some ritual business to dispose of. Each morning, before I settled in, I checked each shelf to see if anything had been sold since the day before. Carl's business was not brisk, and there were days when he did not appear to have sold a single book. This comforted me. I took an almost proprietary interest in his stock, and it pained me to find anything missing. So I would go down each row, scanning the familiar spines, stopping if I spied a gap. There, in U.S. History, a book called *The Indian Wars* had vanished. It was always possible that a careless customer had put it back in the wrong place, or that Carl had sent it out for rebinding. But more likely it was gone for good. I ran my finger over the row, wincing as I passed the closed-up spot. It was like feeling a phantom limb. Once or twice I had tried to make conversation with Carl about these disappearances, thinking he might share my odd sense of loss. But he merely scowled and turned back to his papers. Yet I'd noticed how he behaved whenever he rang up a sale. He would lick his finger and turn the pages of the book very slowly, refusing to give it up until he had sampled it one last time. The customer would begin to shift his feet impatiently, wondering if Carl was going to sell the book after all. And when the transaction was finally complete and the customer had gone out the door Carl would shake his head after him, as if he'd just allowed one of his children to run out to play in traffic.

As always, the last section I checked for changes was Poetry, for one book in particular there meant a great deal to me. It was old and fragile and bound in blue cloth, and I'd first spotted it about ten years earlier. I had never heard of the writer, whose name was Frederick Goddard Tuckerman; the book, dated 1930, was a collection of nature sonnets originally published in the 1860s. I'd pulled out the book and jiggled it gently in my palm, testing it, just as I might test a leaf in Central Park. Its pages were brownish and soft with age, but the binding was still stiff and the book had the feeling of never having been read. I turned to the first sonnet and began. "Sometimes, when winding slow by brook and bower . . ." I almost ended there, before I began; *bower* promised nineteenth-century tedium. I ran my eyes over what was to follow. The style of the sonnets was unabashedly archaic, full of *o'er*s and *thou*s and syntactic tangles. There were stagy references to mythological figures. But I continued all the same, because something in the poems unsettled me.

> On from day to day I coldly creep
> By summer farms and fields, by stream and steep,
> Dull, and like one exhausted with deep sleep.

I had closed the book and stopped reading. Gloom, sterility, dread. I ought to have returned the book to its place and never looked at it again. Yet the next day I went straight to it and, stomach knotted, read some more. Before long it became a compulsion, each day, to read a poem or two from *The Sonnets of Frederick Goddard Tuckerman* before I could start my morning browse. "My proudest thoughts do seem / Bald at the best and dim: a barren gleam." The book did not give me pleasure. I knew that I would never buy it, never want to own it. But each morning I would approach the shelf with a tightness in my chest, afraid that I would find it gone.

I put the book of sonnets back in its place and walked again through all the rows I had just passed through. I kept my eye out for new arrivals, pulled out old favorites, read a paragraph here and another there, fussed with loose bindings, perused the marginal graffiti scrawled by eager readers of the past. Was it history I wanted today, or philosophy? Drama or science? Would my afternoon be spent with one of those fat, flexible Penguin paperbacks that bent double in one's hand, or a library edition, with its ugly but reassuringly authoritative plastic jacket? When I reached Classics I stopped to turn to the famous passage in Plato's *Symposium* in which Aristophanes claims that human beings were once creatures with two sets of arms and legs and genitals but were later punished by the gods by being sliced in two. Ever since, Aristophanes says, we have been seeking our lost other halves, the beings or bodies that would complete us. I read this story often, and there were moments when, half believing it, I longed to go back in time and see such a race of people. Would they move with an infinite flowing grace, like those Indian gods with extra heads and arms?

A customer entered, setting off the bells and causing Carl to make a dry creak in his chair. I glanced at my watch. Marion would soon go off her shift, and I needed a meal. I replaced my book and nodded to Carl's bent head as I went out.

The Stardust Diner, where I ate lunch each day, was in the West Fifties. I liked it for its torn banquettes, the stale mints at the cash register, and Marion. Normally I arrived before noon, when it was not busy, but if the place was more crowded than usual I waited for one of Marion's tables so as not to be served by anyone else. Marion offered no unnecessary chat, no false service smile. Her face was unnaturally tanned and heavily lined, as if she spent long summers in the sun, but never in fifteen years had I known her to take more than a few days' vacation. When she had a minute off her feet, she sat at the counter next to the doughnut stand and drew fiercely on her cigarette. The other waitresses chatted with one another, traded stories about manicures or difficult children. Marion never joined in. Once, when she had been gone for a couple of days, I made the mistake of asking her where she had been. "My daughter had a breast removed," she said, slapping the flatware on the table the same as always, and turned away. A different waitress, ugly Connie with the mole at the corner of her mouth, came to take my order. After that I was more careful of our deal: ask nothing, tell nothing. As long as I obeyed that law, I knew that Marion would appear at my side just when my coffee cup needed a refill, that my one-egg order would arrive with an extra egg at no charge, that my dessert of rice pudding would be heaped high and generously coated with cinnamon.

Today I was so late that the lunch crowd was already gone. I slid into one of Marion's booths and pushed aside a tattered cardboard turkey meant for a centerpiece. Someone in the booth in front of mine, a woman, was crying quietly. Another woman murmured consoling phrases. I stood up to move to a different table, and as I did so my eyes locked with those of the consoling woman. She frowned and I turned away, annoyed that she thought I was eavesdropping. I slid up against the window in the next booth and grabbed a *Village Voice* that someone had left facedown on the table, flipped backward through the classifieds:

> Great oral service! Sexy WF, submissive, seeks
> dominant well-endowed macho man to put her in
> her place.

Handsome hot hugely endowed WM, 32, 6 foot
2, seeks hirsute black pregnant female, my apt.,
daytime, Brooklyn.

Marion appeared over my shoulder and I closed the paper, embarrassed. I set the eviction notice on the table next
to my coffee. *Paul X. Giglio Associates, petitioner to the Civil
Court of the City of New York.* It had yesterday's date on it,
the twenty-ninth of November, and it occurred to me that
my birthday had been on the twenty-seventh. It was the
first time I had thought of it, and I had to stop and ask myself just how old I was. Forty—I had turned forty. I touched
the hot rim of my coffee cup. I had entered a new decade of
life without even noticing. I tried to remember my thirty-
ninth birthday, or my thirty-eighth. Nothing came to mind.

When I was done reading and rereading the court notice I took out my book. It was a medium-sized paperback,
priced at three ninety-five, that I bought at the old Double-
day bookstore on Fifth Avenue during my second year of
law school. I could remember the exact provenance of almost every one of my books, and the cost, too. I turned to
the first page.

Some years ago I was struck by the large number
of falsehoods that I had accepted as true in my
childhood, and by the highly doubtful nature of
the whole edifice that I had subsequently based on
them. I realized that it was necessary, once in the

course of my life, to demolish everything completely
and start again right from the foundations.

I read Descartes's *Meditations*, one of my favorite books,
at least once a year. Each time, I liked to follow Descartes
in his project of beginning with one absolutely indisput-
able truth and rebuilding the universe from it: the natural
world, the life of the mind, even God. Every time, I found
that I snagged on one link of the argument or another, and I
was never sure if Descartes had failed to make his reasoning
airtight or if I had failed to understand something. But each
year I liked to try again, because I too wanted to be able
to take one true thing and from it construct a system that
would allow me to understand everything. I had a fantasy
of finding the perfect book, the one that would illuminate
absolutely all, draw every single fact into a coherent design.
My mother's family would have said that that book was the
Bible, but she had dismissed that answer and I dismissed it
too. Although the *Meditations* failed, like all the others, to
be my perfect book, I had a special fondness for it. Its clear,
confident prose always gave me the illusion, for a time, of
things being in their proper place at their proper time.

The sky had deepened to the color of slate and Marion
had long ago taken my empty rice pudding glass away. A
burst of wind rattled my window. It was late; the daylight
would not linger much longer. Going back to the apartment
this morning had put me hours behind schedule. Depart-
ing from my routine made me unhappy, as if my own skin

did not fit quite right. I paid for my meal, leaving a large tip as always; Marion's tips were one of my few indulgences. As I walked out of the coffee shop I saw, ahead of me, a man with a shaved head nibbling on another man's ear. The shaved man's hand was thrust in the back pocket of the other man's jeans. I watched his brownish tongue emerge, the wet, pointed tip. I thought of the quick rustlings and low moans I sometimes heard in the Ramble. The nibbler, feeling my stare, turned his handsome skull and stuck the tongue out at me. I dropped back, surprised.

By the time I reached the law library it was already dark. Office workers were beginning to move in slack waves toward the buses and subways. At the front desk of the library my old ID card, sixteen years expired, was accepted with a quick nod. I was twenty-two years old when I first walked as a student into these somber rooms with their rows of identical-looking volumes, and now, taking in all of those hundreds of books at one glance, I again experienced the sense of possibility that once made me foolishly decide to become a lawyer. I had loved the study of law, and when graduation had neared and we were pressed to choose a specialty, a professional niche, I settled on trusts and estates. Was it any accident that I was drawn to this? My own challenge to my parents' will languished in the courts as I made my way through school. After graduation I was offered a position at the firm of Watteau & Charles, and at first all went smoothly. Wealthy and important men called Mr. Watteau to praise the smart young lawyer he'd recently hired. More than once I was asked to share Mr. Watteau's table for lunch. But in fact, I was a failure at the job—that is, at doing the work I was asked to do, when I was asked to do it. If a topic interested me I would pursue it tirelessly; I would jump through hoops to solve problems for a client. But anything that seemed routine or uninspiring—and as the months went by more and more did—I would put off until repeated calls sent Mr. Watteau down to my office, where he might find me with a book in hand, my feet up on my desk. Law firms are generous places in their way, and Mr. Watteau really wanted me to succeed. He kept me on for more than a year before firing me for tardiness, unexplained absences, failure to complete assigned projects, and unauthorized reading of Aeschylus and Aristotle.

At the computer terminal I searched for books on New York City rental codes. I'd had to learn to use a computer after my branch library uptown replaced its card catalogue a few years before. For a while the oak drawers sat in crooked heaps by the circulation desk, waiting to be discarded. I thought about asking whether I could bring a couple of them home, but one day all the cards in the drawers were removed and stacked blank side up near the new computers for people to use as scrap. Without the cards the drawers were just furniture to me, devoid of mystique. Sometimes I thumbed through the scrap-paper piles and read the old typed entries. *Heyerdahl, Thor. Early Man and the Ocean. Cox, Claire. The Fourth R: What Can Be Taught about Religion in the Public Schools.*

I sat in a carrel away from a group of chatting students and took notes until the hour to return home drew near. Coming out of the library into the sharp wind, I saw two figures seated on the stone steps below and knew instantly from the matching shapes of the heads that they were twins. My pulse quickened, my fingertips tingled; the universe had again chosen to affirm to me that it dealt in affinities. In an attempt to prolong the moment I walked past the two figures and turned on the half-lit steps. What I saw startled me. They were two boys, perhaps fourteen or fifteen years old, with the wide soft faces and sloe eyes that signal Down syndrome. They held hands. Their dark blazers and white button-down shirts had the look of a school uniform. They seemed to be waiting for someone; their postures were patient, trusting. I wondered if their caretaker was coming for them soon. It seemed impossible to me that the boys did not have someone to look after them, but the minutes passed and no one arrived.

I checked my watch; there was still time to catch my usual train. One of the boys said something to the other in a high-pitched voice and his brother laughed like someone who doesn't understand a joke but pretends he has. I wondered if I should call the police. I thought of being home with a book in my hand and the sharp aroma of my coffee at my side. The more I thought of the train and the book and the coffee, the more certain I became that the police would take a long while to come, and when they finally did come they would ask suspicious questions. And how did I know that the mother or teacher wasn't right around the corner, rushing back from some errand, all apologies? The police officers would stand around me as I explained with rising urgency that I needed to go, that I had the 6:27 train to catch. That I had nothing to do with the boys, could do nothing about them. Somehow I would have become re-sponsible for them, and it would be my fault if they came to grief. Or the mother would arrive and begin to shout at me, to accuse me of having embarrassed her, of poking my nose into business not my own.

The wind tore loose with an audible howl, and one of the boys whimpered. My heart jumped and I knew that things were not all right, that the mother was not just around the corner, that the police, if they came, would never find her. At the same time I thought of the train, my train, racing past the station. I hurried toward the subway and made it onto the platform just as my train pulled in. Out of the corner of my eye I saw the sign posted near the turnstile: STARTING 12:00 AM ON JANUARY 1, THIS STATION WILL NO LON-GER ACCEPT TOKENS. It was the same sign that had gone up earlier in the month at the Broadway-Nassau station. PLEASE USE ONLY METROCARD AFTER THIS DATE. An-other unnecessary, incomprehensible change! Across from me the woman with the beige purse turned her face away.

Five

This afternoon my "work practice," or chore, is to rake the dry garden. Although at other times I have been sent to wash pots in the kitchen or tear boards from a dilapidated garage, increasingly I am given what gardening work becomes available. For two days I turned up the cold earth in the vegetable garden and last week I was sent in a taxi to purchase seeds and dirt from the nursery in nearby Conklin. Afterward a woman monk and I started some basil and squash and put them in a sunny room off the kitchen. When I have a rare moment to myself I slip inside and mark their progress.

The dry garden is a large bed of gravel, bordered by shrubs and dead grass, into which irregular clusters of large stones have been set. There is a stone bridge and a stone lantern. We are supposed to clear away branches and other debris that the winter has deposited and then rake the gravel into wavelike patterns meant to represent water. The illusion, murmured the monk who walked us over, should be of a gently rippling pond. He told us that the dry garden is among the spots the abbot favors for meditation.

The moment my rake cuts three parallel lines into the stone I recognize where I am: inside the picture I saw the day I waited for Patrick outside the Chelsea Zen Center, the picture in the brochure. The photograph had been taken at such close range that all I had been able to make out then was a swirl, a grainy abstract pattern. But now the code is broken; the image was not abstract after all but a part of something real: rocks, gravel, grass. This unveiling, this new piece of meaning, makes me for a moment inordinately happy.

Another man has been sent to work with me, a tall man with scarred skin who introduces himself as Roger. I have never seen him before; he does not share my room. I nod and manage to spit out my own name, glad for the work-practice rule that prohibits any further conversation between us. We are supposed to concentrate only on the motion of raking, on the scratchy sound the gravel makes as it is loosened, the vibrations that travel through the metal teeth up through the wooden pole and into the arm. I fall into a pleasant rhythm of stroke and pause, stroke and pause. At one point, absorbed in our work, Roger and I back into each other and twist away in a shimmy of mutual embarrassment. After this my raking is jerky and self-conscious. I catch one foot under the teeth of my rake and stumble. When a dark shape approaches I am glad for an excuse to stop a moment and see who it is.

It is Joku, toiling up the hill. When he reaches the garden bed he tells me he wants me to come with him to the bonsai shed. I lay my rake in the grass and follow, my eyes trailing his feet. He is wearing the kind of shoes one would expect a monk to wear: dark, thick-soled leather sandals, humble, earth-hugging shoes. I notice that the backs are worn down much farther on one side than on the other. His gait must be lopsided. I am surprised that in this weather he does not wear socks. His heels are calloused, flaky, gray. I look away.

We walk for several minutes, until Joku ducks his head to enter a windowed shed not far from the abbey. My nostrils take in a smell of dust and clay. The room is filled with bonsai plants—on shelves, on the floor, crowded on large tables. There are more of them, and they look even worse, more dried out and scraggly, than Joku had led me to expect.

Since our conversation in the dining hall I have tried to remember anything I can about bonsai. They are most commonly conifers or evergreens, at times quince, crab apple, maple, or dog rose. The art of bonsai originated in China around the twelfth century. But little of practical use has come to me. I mumble something to Joku about how the plants need to be bare-rooted and repotted. The word *bare-rooted* sounds esoteric to my ears, persuasive. I open drawers, looking for tools. I find some chopsticks, shears in different sizes, a kitchen knife, a kind of claw with two metal prongs. I hold up the claw, say that it can be used to pull the dirt off the root-ball. "Ah, I see," says Joku, and asks whether I have everything that I need.

I make a show of looking for more supplies, and then tell him that I do. But Joku has not come empty-handed. He offers me a book, saying that he got it out of the abbey library, in case I should need something for reference. *The Art of Bonsai*, it is called, and I begin to page through it, my spirits rising. There are long columns of print on types of soils and methods of pruning, with big glossy pictures for illustration. I read eagerly, then recall Joku's presence and riffle through the rest of the pages as if the information is familiar to me. Joku walks about the room inspecting the plants, making concerned noises. I find myself afraid that he will topple a pot, trample on a trailing branch. I am glad when he goes out.

But as soon as he is gone I again see clearly what is around me. The plants really have been badly handled. Some pots are cracked where roots have struggled their way out, and the crowns of the trees are leggy, shaggy, drooping with their own weight. I page through the book again, disheartened.

Six

The deadline passed for me to remove myself from my apartment, but there were no more notices. I did not know whether the reprieve would be short or long; in the meantime I kept to my usual activities, enjoying the pretense that all was as it had been before. I let my visits to the law library taper off. The most pressing of my concerns, for many days, was the transition from tokens to electronic cards at the Broadway-Nassau station. I spent some precious time checking other stations in the neighborhood and eventually found that Cortlandt Street would continue to accept tokens. I thought about changing my route so that I could return home each evening from there. But that would mean having to switch trains at Herald Square. I tried to imagine the unfamiliar train, possibly with a different kind of hand bar or seat configuration, the unfamiliar route, the absence forevermore of the briefcase man and the purse lady. I thought of the transfer at Herald Square, of having to push against the late-rush-hour crowds, and I gave up on the idea. One morning, therefore, I bought one of the new cards, to give myself time to get used to it. It was yellow and had a thick black magnetic stripe at the bottom. At the top, blue letters rising as if heading off into the distance read *MetroCard*.

I watched other commuters, to see what they did at the new turnstiles, and after a while I too went to swipe the card through the narrow slot. The turnstile gave a little jolt and refused to let me pass. I ran the card through again, and again I was jolted back. Perhaps, I thought, my card didn't work. A middle-aged man, seeing my perplexity, stopped and showed me that I was holding the card backward, that the magnetic stripe had to face left and not right. I thanked him and this time successfully pushed the card through, but all the same I felt that there could only be trouble ahead, that I would never grow comfortable with this new system. I turned and exited back through the turnstile, and the man who had helped me looked at me with surprise. But I had only been making a trial run. I put the card in my wallet and hoped that I would remember how much it was worth: three more rides. It bothered me that there was nothing on the card itself to indicate this. I climbed back up to street level, fingering the tokens, still usable for now, in my pocket. The round perimeters felt reassuringly thick under my thumb.

As the days went by I tried to decide whether or not Giglio was moving ahead with his renovation plans. The signs weren't clear. One evening I returned home to find the vacated ground-floor apartment open, its living room lined with plastic sheets. Opposite my own front door a large and seemingly purposeless hole had been punched into the wall, and plaster dust had been swept into a tall pyramid beside it. Was it a warning, an attempt at harassment? I waited to see. Day after day the pyramid sat there, growing neither larger nor smaller, until Mrs. Fiore came to sweep it up. After their single day of activity, she told me, the workmen had not returned. But the architect—*Patrick*, she called him— had stopped by and dropped off some herbs for her. She had wrapped them in cheesecloth and steeped them in boiling water—he'd given her directions half a mile long, she said, so serious about it all—but she was damned if it had done anything for her pain. I could see, though, that she'd been flattered by his attention. I changed the subject, annoyed that I'd missed him, and did not admit that I too had begun to call him Patrick in my thoughts. In imagination I saw him again at dusk at the entranceway, and he told me he had forgotten to take certain measurements, certain photographs. He needed, he said, to see my apartment again. On the way up the stairs, leading him, I would stumble and his hand would fly out to brace my side, but I would right myself before he reached me. Anxiously he would ask if I was all right. *Yes*, I would assure him. *I'm all right.*

Midmonth we had a few balmy days that seemed to wilt the paper Santas pasted to the storefront windows and take the shine off the Christmas baubles hanging from the lampposts, but afterward it turned sharply cold again, and when

I emerged in the mornings for my walk to the park, Mrs. Fiore was sometimes waiting on the stairs for me, bundled up in an ankle-length down coat with an old scarf wound around her head. Her face expressed reproach, as much of me as of our landlord. Deep in the bowels of city government lay powers of law that could put things to right—if only I would set them in motion. *We could beat him*, she was saying with her long-suffering face, *but you must help. I'm just a woman; I can't do it myself.* Each time I greeted her politely and walked on, pretending that I did not see her silent demand. Had I ever led her to believe I was a man of action, a fixer? Had I ever misled her?

Two nights before Christmas I was awakened by a banging at my door, repeated, urgent. "Coming!" I called. "All right, coming!" Then it struck me that a visitor at this hour could mean nothing good, and I shoved my feet into a pair of shoes and searched for something large and menacing to hold in my hands. Giglio—it had to be Giglio. No, not him but two men he had hired who would grab me and knock me down to teach me a lesson. Helplessly I ran from sofa to bookcase and finally seized the fireplace poker. The pounding continued, and beneath it I heard Mrs. Fiore's pleading voice. I opened the door. In the brightness of the hallway her back receded down the stairs, and I followed her. I had a vague impression of heat above my head, an extra density in the atmosphere, but I saw nothing, smelled nothing, not then. Mrs. Fiore moved so quickly that before I knew it I was out on the street, looking up at my darkened balcony, which held my uncle's clay planters that I had never removed nor tended to but that every spring miraculously flowered with weeds. The cold cut my face. Above my balcony were the lit windows of Mrs. Fiore's front room, and, above that, a murky glow in Mr. Flax's old apartment. I had always thought that fire meant bright tongues of flame, smoke billowing from windows. This was mute, subdued.

Mrs. Fiore stood with pursed lips. When she spoke, her voice trembled.

"Arson," she said. "Giglio got tired of waiting."

"No, Frances," I said—the name just slipped out. "Why would you think that?"

Mrs. Fiore turned to me and I was frightened by her face, which looked bloodless and defeated in the half darkness. Her hair, tangled from sleep, looked like the hair of a crazy woman. Her eyes were so dark I couldn't find the irises. "Your uncle never lifted a finger for anyone," she said.

I stuttered out some baffled reply—what did she mean?—but she turned away to the glowing windows and said no more.

I have trouble remembering exactly what happened after that. The firemen came; they threw blankets over us, dingy quilted cloths of the kind that movers throw over bureaus and sideboards. I was still clutching the fireplace poker. I remember a fireman asking us to go to the nearest doorman building to warm ourselves, but neither Mrs. Fiore nor I abandoned our watch. We stood side by side waiting for any sign that the flames were creeping down to the lower floors. At some point windows had to be smashed, and the water from the hoses froze when it hit the stone, leaving a moss of rime. Still, in less than half an hour the fire was out, and when the men returned to tell us the news their impassive faces seemed to express contempt for the flames for putting up such a poor fight. They suspected some bad wiring on the fourth floor, they said; who was our land-lord? Did we have friends or relatives we could stay with for the night? Mrs. Fiore called her daughter on one of the truck phones. "Two days before Christmas!" she shrieked. One of the men turned to me. "And you, sir? Do you have some place to stay?" I had no place, of course, but I only told him that I didn't mind returning to my apartment. The men conferred. The smell was strong, they said, and there were broken windows. They wouldn't advise it.

I meant to stay, I repeated. The one who had just spoken raised his eyebrows. All right, he told me. If that was what I wanted.

At some point a fireman offered to go upstairs and get clothing for Mrs. Fiore to take to her daughter's, but she waved him off, muttering. When her taxi arrived she got into it, a small, nightgown-clad figure, and she did not bid me goodbye. But as the cab pulled away she stopped the driver and called after me to ask if I would shut the door to her apartment. Her daughter, she said, would come after the holiday to get her things. I nodded.

The fire trucks drove off and I went inside. Immediately I was assaulted by a smoky, chemical stench. It settled into my lungs and scraped at the back of my throat, left a taste of plastic in my mouth. I grew winded as I climbed the stairs, and my eyes watered. When I reached Mrs. Fiore's door I hesitated, my hand on the knob, wondering how to delay the finality of shutting the place up forever. I nudged the door open a bit farther and peered inside.

The lights were blazing and on the television a set of kitchen knives silently rotated on a dais, the asking price flashing underneath. I stepped over the threshold, blinking. A large wall mirror caught my approach and I drew back as if I'd been captured on a surveillance camera. Turning away from the glass, I saw that Mrs. Fiore's living room was furnished not so much with chairs and tables as with photographs: photographs propped or mounted on every conceivable surface, on the walls, even hanging by wire from the necks of lamps. I stepped closer. There were pictures of children, teenagers, adults, and old people. The walls held large formal shots, the tables and sideboards smaller and more informal ones. There were pictures taken on beaches, at picnics, in front of houses, in restaurants, at weddings and graduations. There was a series of photographs of young men in military uniform, some in black and white, others, more recent, in color. A young woman with long hair and a wide smile waved from the driver's seat of a 1950s-style Buick. It was Mrs. Fiore, I was suddenly sure. I felt as if I had stumbled into an enormous family reunion. Exactly how many grandchildren, or great-grandchildren, did Mrs. Fiore have? There seemed to be several dozen. I

stood clutching the ridiculous poker, wondering which of
the hundreds of faces might be that of the daughter in Neptune, New Jersey. The images seemed to shimmer and blur.
Beneath the pervasive burnt-chemical odor the apartment
smelled, I realized, of soup. There was a small Christmas
tree in the corner, plastic by the look of it—I could not bring
myself to walk in any farther. My feet were sunk into a shag
rug whose faded rust color made me think of Mrs. Fiore's
hair. I could see through a half wall the cooking range in the
kitchen, each burner covered with a saucepan as if at the
ready for company. Something on the floor above fell with
a loud bang, a delayed casualty of the fire. The feeling of being watched returned to me. I backed out of the apartment
and shut the door.

In my dream I saw the car accident that killed my mother
and father, saw the dark-blue sedan come out of nowhere
and fling their car into a ditch off the highway, where it
turned over and burst into flames. In real life there had been
no fire. My parents had died from the impact, the coroner
had said, my mother instantly, my father more slowly. They
had been traveling home on the Henry Hudson Parkway
after a dinner party when a darting car sideswiped them. In
the dream I left the car where it was, belly-up and burning,
and walked a long way, back to our apartment. I crawled
into my boyhood bed and, exhausted, went to sleep. But
a knocking at the door kept awakening me. Finally I got
up to answer it. It was my mother, warning me that there

was a fire. Because I had not come in time her dress had burst into flames. I saw her spinning and twirling down the staircase, bits of blackened cloth rising from her body, and I knew it would be dangerous to follow.

"That's all right," she said, sitting on the edge of my bed. "I didn't die after all. I'll read to you." Then I was awake, and I lay shivering, my lungs and nostrils thick with a noxious coating. For a moment I really had been a child again and my mother was putting me to bed before she went out for the evening. The dress in the dream was one I remembered, a sheath of shimmery emerald green, off the shoulder, that made her appear to be some sort of mermaid. Every now and then she would read to me from her grandmother's Bible: Adam and Eve, Noah's Ark, Ruth and Naomi, David and Jonathan, all those stories of matched sets. Whenever she readied herself for an evening out, her eyes were bright and she looked beautiful, not at all the way she appeared during the day. After kissing me with her cool lips she would sweep out to join my father and begin their evening, which might start at 10:00 PM at an actor's or producer's home and end with the maid waking them for a noon breakfast.

I threw a bathrobe over my sleep-damp clothing and went into the kitchen to rinse the ashen coating from my mouth. It was past eight o'clock and I would have to move quickly to make up for lost time. It felt strange to be indoors when the sun was so far up in the sky. I drank a glass of water, then another, and was about to brew some coffee when I heard a sound in the stairwell. Patrick's step was already familiar to me and I came out onto the landing. As soon as he caught sight of me I remembered that I was not yet dressed.

"Hello, Mr. Gorse," he said. "Are you all right?"

I nodded. His head was dusted with snow and, feeling giddy, I pointed at it. He reached up, checking, and brought his hand down wet.

"Yes," he said, breaking into a smile. "I guess we're going to have a white Christmas."

He was taller than I remembered, more angular and awkward-looking than the man who in my imagination reached out to brace my fall and ran his hands again over the chairs and curtains in my apartment. I looked at the glittering crystals in his hair and thought about how children were always being told that no two snowflakes are alike. Somewhere, I was sure, I had read otherwise. I believed otherwise. Trillions upon trillions of flakes fall to earth in a single snowfall, and there are tens of thousands of snowfalls each year around the globe. How could one of any kind of snowflake be anything but an accident, a deviation?

Patrick gestured up the stairs apologetically, explaining that Mr. Giglio had sent him to take a look at the damage. He started up and I followed. In the night I had not noticed the dirt and debris the firemen had left behind. We stepped carefully, made our way slowly. "Good Lord," Patrick said. At the top landing, one long wall had been disemboweled. Spongy blackened material spilled out of it, some of it fused to the floor. There were patterns on the walls where the smoke had licked upward, leaving the impression of tall stenciled leaves. Broken glass powdered under our feet. Patrick took out his camera and snapped pictures, then entered Mr. Flax's vacated apartment, from which a frigid draft blew. I waited outside, peeking in at the blackened carpet and shattered windows. Patrick was shaking his head as he came out. "Thank God it wasn't your place," he said, and just then I noticed something odd about the way he was dressed. One untucked tail of his shirt rode above the other; the right and left sides of his collar were out of joint. Patrick noticed me staring and gazed down at himself. "Oh," he said.

"Would you like a cup of coffee?" I blurted out. It was the shirt that made me say it; the clumsiness of it emboldened me. Patrick started to work on the buttons. I wondered if I'd been too abrupt, spoken too loudly. But Patrick raised his head gratefully and said that he would. Mr. Giglio had called him first thing that morning, and he hadn't even taken the time for breakfast.

He nodded as he entered my apartment, as if reminding himself that he had already been here. In the kitchen he was too polite to take the one chair for himself. He leaned against the counter and I had to brush against him to get the coffee filter and the tin of grounds from the cupboard. Delicately he raised one shoe and pried an inch-and-a-half-long shard of glass from a tread. I pressed myself into a corner, holding the filter and the tin. Through the kitchen window I saw the snow falling softly on the cars and the sidewalks. I turned on the oven, hoping that it would quickly warm the room.

After filling the filter with grounds, I realized that I was not sure how to make the second cup of coffee. Should I tip more grounds into the filter and pour in twice as much water? But then the mug would overflow. I couldn't use two separate filters, because I had only one filter holder. I stood for a moment in some confusion. Then I gave the coffee canister a hard rap, filling the filter to the brim, and poured the boiling water over the grounds. When it was done dripping I poured half the coffee into a separate mug and added water to fill it to the top. Handing it to him, I again became aware of my bathrobe, the stubble on my cheeks, the fact that I had not bathed.

A musical jingling erupted from somewhere and Patrick rummaged in his pocket. I had grown used to phones ringing on the street, to people passing by with hidden earpieces talking as if to themselves, but I was startled by the sudden appearance in my kitchen of a third party. "Hello?" he asked softly. "No, I'm on a project visit. That's all right. No, it's really all right. I can be there in an hour."

He closed the phone with a click. "I'm sorry, where were we?"

But we hadn't been speaking. I ducked my head and busied myself dumping the used filter into the garbage can. From his manner it was unclear whether he'd been speaking to a client or a boss or a wife. I moved jerkily from garbage to sink, avoiding Patrick's eyes.

I heard him put down his mug. "May I ask you something?" he said. "Please don't feel you have to say yes." I turned. "Would it be all right," he asked, "if I took your picture?"

Before I could even answer he raised his palms as if to ward off any negative reaction. His fingers were slender, naked—no wedding ring. Only if I felt comfortable, he insisted, only if I wanted to. It was just that I had an interesting face.

But already I was stammering my agreement. "I'd better go change," I said.

"No, stay as you are."

He put his palm on my back to encourage me to stand up straighter. I grew dizzy, closed my eyes, opened them again. He pushed a spoon and a salt shaker to the end of the counter, out of the frame, and adjusted my shoulders. "Relax," he said. He stood back and drew close again. The room was growing very warm and I would have liked to turn off the oven. When Patrick finally raised the camera I involuntarily stiffened. He frowned. "Take a breath and let it out," he said. "Good, now again." But still he did not look pleased. He rotated me into a slightly different position. I had the feeling that something had gone wrong, that I was somehow ruining the photograph. I did my best to smile, but Patrick gently told me to drop any attempt at an expression. Finally he seemed satisfied and I held my face still for the camera. Patrick took one photograph, then several more in rapid succession.

Afterward we stood awkwardly. It seemed I had surrendered something to him, and I was startled by my impulsiveness. I turned and flicked off the oven. Then, light-headed, I shoved my hands deep into the pockets of my robe. Patrick had again picked up his coffee mug and was blowing on it, though surely it was cold by now. That bracelet of his dangled from his wrist, a primitive thing, brown beads on a rough leather thong, tied with a simple knot. And before I could stop myself I had asked him what it was. I was sure he would say that his girlfriend had made it, his fiancée.

Patrick raised his arm, and the sparse blond hairs on it caught the light. "They're Buddhist beads," he said. "We use them in prayer."

"You're a Buddhist?" I mumbled. The girlfriend, the fiancée, disappeared.

He laughed. "I never feel able to say that," he told me. "It's like saying you're an artist, or a saint. You aim at it; you don't ever manage to be it."

He fingered the beads as if for reassurance, and in that moment I saw in him someone I'd once known, a childhood friend named Henry. I was surprised I hadn't thought of it before. The blond hair, the awkward, eager gestures, the bracelet: they were all reminiscent of Henry.

"I meditate at this place near my office," Patrick said. "I try to go nearly every day."

He turned and put his coffee mug into the sink. It clinked against the porcelain. The warmth was quickly fading from the room. Patrick rubbed his arms vigorously and thanked me. It was, he said, getting to be time for him to go.

Seven

Each day I return to the shed with the bonsai and the smell of dust and pine. My new responsibilities are a gift, allowing me an hour or two of solitude and some exemption from the daily routine. Sometimes I overstay my allotted time and do not appear for the afternoon meditation. To my surprise, no one takes me to task for my absence or even questions it. I used to wake in the night wondering whether my residency was running out, whether I would soon be asked to leave the monastery. No one ever said anything about it. But when I began to work with the bonsai I worried a little less. I felt that if I could succeed with the plants I might be seen as useful, at least for a while.

Today I am working on a spruce tree growing in a rectangular container. Its trunk has a deep curve that was trained into it long ago. I wonder who the monk who took care of these plants was, and when and why he left. The spruce has a spiky, disorderly crown and dense growth beneath the branches, in violation of the principle that bonsai growth should be above the branches only, in the direction of heaven. I press back some branches to see how the tree will look if I open up more space at the top. Then I stand at a distance and look at the tree from different angles. I begin to see how this plant might grow, the shapes it might assume. The trunk wants, I think, to bend back against itself, to make an S. Wants? I ask myself. When did a plant ever choose to grow in a particular shape?

With each specimen I have gotten better at my work. I loosen the sides of the plant with a flat tool and remove the impacted rectangle. Thick white roots like veins bulge beneath the surface. I slice off the bottom and sides of the rectangle with a long knife and then scrape away at the soil between the roots until only a small ball of root and dirt is left. With scissors I cut back the longer, dangling roots.

Now I place the plant back into its container. The plant will grow but it will never have more room to spread than this. I am reminded of the Chinese custom of binding little girls' feet to make them fit the same size shoes year after year. I shift the plant this way and that, deciding where to position the root-ball in the pot. Bonsai are never supposed to be perfectly centered. I fill the pot with soil and gravel, using a chopstick to push the dirt down into the spaces between the remaining roots. Now it is time to clean up the plant itself. I pinch a few new buds with my fingers, toss them into the bucket near my feet. I lop off branches that interfere with the shape I have determined upon. Some of them have grown thick and tough and I have to saw at them with a kitchen knife.

Next comes the wiring. The spruce is too mature for me to be able to bend it by hand. The book tells me to begin by using a root cutter to make two gashes in the trunk. Spruce, fortunately, heal quickly. I cut the trunk and grab hold of it with one fist. With the other I take a pair of pliers and slowly press the trunk away from itself, toward the S shape I now see clearly in my mind.

When I first tried to bend a trunk in this way—I'd been working with a juniper—the tree snapped beneath the pliers and I was left with a jagged blade of wood, the foliage flung to the ground several feet away. I picked up the severed bunch of leaves and threw it away with a shudder. I felt an extraordinary sense of wrongdoing. The trunk I could not bring myself to throw away. I left it on the worktable, near me, as a reminder to be more careful, to go slow.

I wrap wire around the trunk, securing it to the side of the pot. Now I move to the branches, and I raise or lower these and secure them with more wire. Each time I make a change I discover other changes that need to follow, intrusive branches or superfluous buds, and I go on in this way until only the fear of being left with nothing—only the idea of a plant, not the plant itself—stops me.

My book emphasizes that wiring is highly traumatic for the plant. Afterward it must be watered, placed away from direct sunlight, and left alone for several days. It gives me an odd feeling, all this forcing and tying. I am light-headed and a little nauseated afterward. I feel sorry for the plants; I put them on the cool dim shelves and turn my eyes away. Supposedly I am making the plants resilient and strong, and if that is really true I can count on their outliving me by decades, maybe even centuries.

Eight

I suppose I'd played with other children before Henry; I must have. But I remember only Henry. I recall building a block castle with some other, now faceless boy, but what has fixed this incident in memory all these years is not the castle, which I can't picture any more than I can picture the boy, but the unusually pleasant scent that drifted out of the kitchen while we were playing and that distracted me until I insisted on going downstairs to see what it was. There sat the two maids, his and mine, chatting over butter cookies and some unusual type of tea the other maid must have brought with her. The other maid smiled and asked in her Islands accent if I wanted any cookies. I stuffed three into my mouth at once, surprising even myself. They dissolved against my tongue into a velvety mush. Our maid—I think it was Anita at that time, the names and faces were always changing—told me I was being rude but her companion waved her hand dismissively and said sweet butter was good for any boy. Because of the maid I was eager to play with the boy again but on his next visit someone different was with him. I must have been very unfriendly because he never came to the house again. Mostly I liked to play alone.

The summer I was thirteen, my parents rented a house in the Adirondacks for the season, a cabin with big exposed timbers and a stone fireplace. I can't imagine what inspired them to take the place, for neither of them enjoyed the country. They lived for theater and parties and the city. My father never did come out on the weekends to stay with my mother and me. He remained in Manhattan, keeping track of the theaters he owned and his related businesses. He kept the maid with him, and for the first time my mother was without the help of housekeeper, cook, or driver. At first I was delighted to have my mother all to myself, but it soon became clear that my ideas of canoe rides and cookouts with her would not be fulfilled. She slept much of the time and smoked cigarette after cigarette, leaving full ashtrays all over the house which I eventually emptied. She read fat novels which fell into the bathtub when she dozed off and later turned up, swollen, in the trash.

One morning she walked me down to the nearest neighbor's, half a mile away. I didn't want to go; I wanted to keep an eye on her and wait for her to come around enough to play a board game or cards with me. But when Henry appeared, after being called to the door, something earnest and shy about him prevented me from keeping my eyes rebelliously fixed on the ground. He was about the same height as I was, with serious eyes and a smiling mouth and blond hair that curled below his ears. His mother, plump and affable, ordered him to take me to his room. There he showed me a homemade camera and some glassine packages containing beetles and bugs. I was instantly envious of this orderly and carefully labeled collection and asked him to explain all about the fixative he had used to prevent the bugs from disintegrating. Then he showed me the frog he kept in a glass tank.

"My aim in life," he said, "is to discover a brand-new species of something. I don't care what it is—it could even be mold. And then I would name it after me."

Finally Henry's mother flushed us out of the room with scooping motions of her hands, asking us how we would ever become great scientists if we never went out of the house. I was startled by her big gestures and round sloppy body and the hint of mockery in everything she said; she was so entirely different from my mother. We hiked down into the ravine, where Henry collected leaves and bugs. Several times I wanted to go back, thinking the ravine was too steep, but Henry insisted that he'd help me; he did this all the time. He showed me the bracelet he wore, a leather strap with a metal disk hanging from it. The disk was engraved with the name and serial number of an older cousin who was fighting in Vietnam. He would wear it, he said, until his cousin came home safely. When he spoke about Vietnam his eyes grew even more serious than usual and his voice deepened. I found myself wishing that I were his cousin, doing something dramatic far away from home, longed for and worried over.

That summer had begun cold and rainy, and in the mornings I often curled up shivering in my bed, not wanting to wake. But Henry got up and out early and would knock on my door, catapulting me into alertness. I threw on my clothes and we would go out to catch salamanders or just to trek silently through the woods, idly slapping at the trees with the branches we carried. Once, in one of the puddles that collected in the muddy trails and did not disappear for weeks, I saw a bulbous brownish object that I instantly took for the excrement of some large animal. I stepped back, disgusted. Henry laughed and poked at the thing with a stick. It went under the surface and bobbed up again. I began to think it wasn't excrement after all: light gleamed on its surface and made it semitransparent. What is it? I asked. Henry told me that it was a great sac of frog eggs, that in a few weeks the tadpoles would emerge, hundreds of thousands, maybe millions, of them. This answer made me even more queasy, as I pictured millions of tails with large blind heads attached, wriggling and wriggling until the water seethed with their motion.

In mid-July the heat suddenly, scorchingly arrived. The puddles in the road dried up overnight, and I wondered where the egg sacs had gone. Would the tadpoles all die? But Henry promised that when August came we would see tons of frogs leaping in the ponds and hear them calling from the tall grass. He and his mother came up here every summer; it was always the same.

One morning, without speaking about it, Henry and I raced to the pond to go swimming. Henry, as usual, was faster than I was. He clambered onto a rock and stripped off his shirt. Is it possible I had never seen him shirtless before? If I had, I hadn't taken it in. Henry gestured to me to join him. But I could not move. His body transfixed me in its unfamiliarity. It seemed to leap out at me: bold, raw, strange. His chest was skinny, a lattice of bones dotted with patches of eczema. His yellow hair was pasted by perspiration against the sides of his face. His nose was narrow, his eyebrows invisible, his hands delicate. He reached down to pull off his shorts and I turned away.

I clutched my arms around my T-shirt as if the temperature had dropped again. I don't feel well, I called out to him in a thin voice. I sat down in the grass, shivering, my face averted. I heard the splash of Henry entering the water and listened while he clowned around for a while, trying to persuade me to come in, until finally my absence made him feel silly. He began to put his clothes back on and I dizzily stood up to go. On the way back to the main road, as we walked in silence, I tripped over a tree root and bloodied my knee. Henry reached out a hand to help me and when he had me back on my feet I pushed him hard to the ground. He stared at me in surprise, then rose and brushed himself off, and we went on.

When we reached my door I ran into the darkness of my house without saying goodbye. My mother was in her room with her door closed. I lay down on my bed, still dizzy. My head and neck hurt. I slept on and off, waking nauseated and disoriented throughout the morning and afternoon. Late in the day my mother came to check on me, and found me feverish, with dried vomit on my bedspread. When I failed to get better after several days a doctor was called in and announced to my mother that I had viral meningitis. I was in bed for a couple of weeks and then slowly I began to recover.

I never saw Henry after that summer, but I still thought about him. I was thinking about him as I washed the dishes after Patrick's departure, wiped the counters, restored the salt shaker to its usual position. Every object seemed more correct when it was back in its proper place. But after dropping the shard of glass Patrick had taken from his shoe into the garbage pail, I changed my mind and took it out again. I was holding it, wondering what to do with it, when I noticed that Patrick had left his camera on the kitchen chair.

I picked it up and unzipped the case. The camera was sleekly silver and surprisingly light. I pressed a button and a lens pushed out, a buzzing, perky robotic snout. I turned the snout toward me and peered into it, as if, if I looked hard enough, I could glimpse inside the pictures Patrick had made of me. I drew my thumb slowly over the grainy silver sheath.

I wondered how far he would get before he noticed—three or four blocks? halfway across the city? Surely he would turn right back. I settled myself on the couch to read while I waited for him but found I could not anchor my thoughts. At this hour I was usually making my way into the Ramble. Snow would be falling on the sassafras and the viburnum and dusting the asphalt paths. Everything would look clean and calm. I cleared my throat and tasted the cindery phlegm.

I wanted to wash. In the bathroom I watched the frigid water spill from the bathtub tap. It was useless to think of a shower; the last time I'd tried one the icy needles falling from overhead had sent me into a gasping dance. I wet a washcloth and scoured myself, teeth gritted, removing my pants and shirt bit by bit, trying to stay covered until the last possible moment. Lately this painstaking routine had made me acutely aware of my body: the looseness of the skin on my thighs, the wiry hair around my groin. Gray hair sprang from my chest. Sometimes, crouched next to the tap, a smell would reach my nostrils, a pungent mulchy odor which I associated with old people, and which I remembered sometimes having detected under my father's cologne.

But once the ordeal of the bath was over there was a heightened enjoyment in dressing for the day. The cold water shocked my skin into a feeling of deep cleanliness, against which the wool of my sweater and socks felt pleasurably abrasive. I put on each article of clothing slowly, as if readying myself for an appointment. When my keys and wallet were in my pocket I glanced at the clock and told myself that I could afford to wait a few minutes longer; it would be a shame if Patrick came back for his camera and

I had just gone out. Perhaps he needed it for the holidays. I waited twenty minutes, and then twenty more. I turned the kitchen oven on again. I walked about the living room, scanned the bookshelves, thumbed through record jackets, looked through my uncle's desk. At the back of one drawer was a slingshot my uncle had given to me on a visit when I was about ten years old. It was solid wood, with a groove down the center and a thick, supple leather strap. When I first saw it I thought it looked like a real weapon, like something a boy in days of old might have used to kill squirrels to skin and eat. My mother turned to my uncle with uncharacteristic disapproval and said, "Come on, now, Fred. He could put a boy's eye out with it." I was horrified: a boy's eye? We left the gift behind, my mother murmuring her apologies, and then, years later, I found it in the drawer, and instantly felt guilty, as if I had in fact injured someone with it.

Most of the drawers in the desk held ledger papers: lists of numbers, budgets. Every so often, as now, I pulled them out and looked at them. In April of 1969 my uncle had spent twenty-two dollars on groceries, two dollars on newspapers, nine dollars on books. May of '69 was not very different. I had found no personal correspondence when I went through my uncle's things after his death, nothing of a personal nature whatsoever, though I know my mother used to get letters from him—letters, although he lived only across the park. "Fred doesn't like the phone," my mother explained to my father. There were all sorts of things, according to her, that Fred liked or didn't like. He liked ice cream. He didn't like holidays. "Like, like," my father answered. "We all know something else that Fred *likes*." My mother frowned and shushed him.

I stood at the window and stared down the block as if I might be able to will Patrick into returning from that direction. The snow was falling more heavily now and bundled figures were hurrying against the swells. The snow sifted onto the cars and the sidewalks, soft and powdery looking, though by morning it would be pushed into crusty banks against the sides of the street and laced with grime and dog urine. Church bells rang in the distance. Wasn't forgetting a form of wishing? I asked myself. Perhaps Patrick had left his camera behind because he hadn't really wanted to leave. If he hadn't wanted to leave then he might return.

I began to pull food out of my kitchen cabinets: a box of crackers, a jar of strawberry jam, a dusty cellophane package of lemon drops I could not remember having acquired. From the refrigerator, a wedge of cheese, an orange. I set these items out on a large plate and arranged them a number of times until they looked sufficiently attractive. Then I went back to waiting. I thought of Carl closing his shop early for Christmas, switching off the aisle lights one by one. Marion would also be leaving early. All over the city, stores were locking up, and the public places, *my* places, the parks and libraries, were emptying. People were boarding planes to their childhood homes or snaking out of town on the lit parkways. It was on one of these parkways, in another

wintertime, that my parents had died. Absently I reached
into the bag of lemon drops and sucked on a candy. I looked
to see if I owned a book about Buddhism, though I knew
I didn't. There was plenty, though, on anarchism: Durruti,
Proudhon, the Haymarket bombing. I had never figured out
what had given my uncle, an accountant, a Quaker by birth,
such an interest in lawlessness. Did he believe that man was
naturally peaceful and good but was warped by brutal social arrangements? Or was it the violent wing of anarchy
that attracted him, the rage and the bombs? I would never
know. When my mother and I made our infrequent visits
here during my childhood (my father always claimed another engagement), my mother talked about the work she
was getting or couldn't get, the difficulties an aging actress
faced, the directors who were giving her trouble, and my
uncle simply praised and encouraged her until she shook
her head, laughing. They never talked about my uncle, what
he did or thought about. At times I recognized how strange
it was that every day I impersonated a man, a blood relative,
who remained a complete mystery to me.

The sun slid beneath the window and darkness came.
At last I turned off the kitchen oven, thinking that I would
pay dearly for the warmth it had given today. I put Patrick's
camera on the mantelpiece. Next to it I placed the shard of
glass from his shoe, then his business card. I sat and looked
at these objects. Then I got up and closed the window curtains, though usually I liked to see the apartments opposite
at night: the glow of desk lamps and computer screens, and

in this season the lighted trees and electric menorahs. A thick dust rose as I drew the fabric.

It was not late, but I changed into my nightclothes and slid between the sheets of my bed. I pulled over myself one blanket, then another, then a third, and finally a thick quilt my uncle had owned. I lay on my back, my hands folded under all these layers, watching the ceiling, thinking that even now I might hear a knock at the door, might open it to find a tall man with a nervous, earnest face, asking if he might come in. And if he did? I wondered. What would I do then?

Nine

One morning I find myself on the top floor of the abbey, looking for a broom. I have rarely been to this floor, which is reserved for the monks and the long-term residents. I get lost, walk down an unfamiliar hallway, pass an open bedroom. Something makes me pause at the doorway and look in. The room is a narrow rectangle furnished only with a cot, a small desk, a lamp, and a chair, but in its privacy it seems magnificent to me. The cot is neatly made and yet askew, the sheets tucked in at something of an angle instead of evenly on each side. A dark sock peeks from between the cot and its frame. When I squint I can see that the small bookshelf propped on the desk holds volumes by Freud, Winnicott, Lacan.

I am sure that this is Joku's room, and not only because of the hint of untidiness strenuously controlled. In the dining hall I once heard him explain to someone that his mother

had died when he was only a few months old. He said that
from the moment he was conscious of himself he knew that,
unlike other little boys, he had no mommy. He knew that
life was about missing something, desiring something—
something you want so much you'll die without it. That was
why he'd become a psychoanalyst.

I step into the room. There is a library in the abbey, but
it is filled with titles like the *Platform Sutra of the Sixth Pa-
triarch* and *The Flower Ornament Scripture*. Now that I am
closer to the shelves I note that Joku has several volumes of
Western poetry and philosophy in addition to the books
on psychology. I have just opened *The Psychopathology of
Everyday Life* when Joku speaks to me from the doorway.

"Do my books interest you?"

He waves away my startled and guilty expression. It's
all right, he tells me. He leaves his door open as a kind of
discipline, so that he has no impulse to privacy, to self-
withholding and secrets. If he invites trespassers, he must
expect them occasionally. He drops into the chair and motions me to sit on the bed.

"That's my favorite Freud," he says. "There's nothing more
interesting, is there, than everyday life. Mistakes, oversights,
misunderstandings. Every day we testify against ourselves."

I acknowledge that it's an interesting book.

"You've read it, then? Do you believe, like Freud, that
there are no accidents, that we intend everything we do?"

I say that I'm not sure. To change the subject, I ask him
why he no longer practices psychoanalysis.

He hesitates, toys with the belt on his robe. "My patients always expected me to end their suffering," he says. "You can't end suffering. That's what Buddhism knows."

If I were to stretch out on the bed right now Joku would be seated behind me, just like the analyst he used to be. Perhaps I would begin to tell him things. But there is no time even to imagine that because we both hear a light knock on the open door and look up to see a woman holding a camera.

Joku greets her and explains that she has come today to take pictures for the summer brochure. Her name is Kim. Kim, a woman of about forty-five with loose long hair and no makeup, waves hello to me. In her long skirt and over-sized sweater, she resembles many of the female residents here. I am trying to decide whether I'm supposed to make some pleasantry or whether I am just supposed to leave, when a flash goes off. I am stunned and lift my hand to ward off the explosion, which has already passed.

Kim backs up to get another angle with her camera.

"No more, please," says Joku, waving her away. "Go and get some of the pretty faces out there. There's a group at the teahouse right now. I'll meet you there shortly."

When Kim is gone Joku says that he's glad we have a few minutes; the abbot has asked him to speak to me. He wants to know what my plans are.

So it has finally come; the abbot's charity is running dry. I murmur the response I have prepared over the days and weeks. Perhaps, I suggest, the abbey could use a full-time gardener. I already care for the bonsai, and I work daily with both the vegetables and the ornamental plants. Everyone seems pleased with my work. The outside service the abbey employs to handle the landscaping must be expensive. It would save money to use me instead. I would stay on, as an employee, but I would not expect to be paid, just to be supplied with my room and board.

Joku looks puzzled. "Do you have nowhere at all to go?"

"No."

His eyes grow anxious. He stands up, smoothing his robe, and says that he will speak to the abbot. Then he asks me if I want to borrow the book.

I have forgotten all about Freud, still clutched in my hand. I shake my head, give it over. It doesn't contain any of the answers I need.

Ten

I awakened at dawn on Christmas Day after a broken sleep and looked out onto the empty street, anxious to go out. The snowplows had been through, but on the cars and balconies the snow still looked unexpectedly pretty and fresh. My eyes stung and I coughed blackened flecks into a tissue. Coffee seemed only to intensify the taste of ash. When I shut off the kitchen tap there was perfect silence in the room, in the entire building, and yet I had the uneasy sense that somewhere the walls were still secretly smoldering, still issuing smoky poisons. I brushed my teeth twice, then bathed.

Central Park West was bare of pedestrians, the air cold but less dry and bitter than the air inside my apartment. There was something hospitable in the atmosphere, an invitation. I could see thirty blocks north to Morningside Heights and twenty blocks south to Columbus Circle, where an electronic display atop a tall building blinked out the temperature and the time. Except for an occasional car jolting past, it was quiet. Holiday mornings—Thanksgiving, Christmas, New Year's—always had this feel about them for me, as if overnight the people who lived in the apartment buildings had been stolen away and only the caretakers were left: the doormen shoveling snow, the garbagemen claiming bags. I walked downtown enjoying this feeling of emptiness, lazily studying the salt-whitened surface of the road, the dirty stone facades, a banner advertising a show at the New-York Historical Society. I rolled a lemon drop over and over in my mouth. When I reached the southernmost entrance to the park, Merchants' Gate, I finally turned toward the green. Merchants' Gate, Scholars' Gate, Farmers' Gate, Engineers' Gate: the names are carved into the stone wall circling the park, Olmsted's tribute to the people whose labors built the city. Olmsted fought for the simplicity of these entrances, mere gaps in the wall, against the artists and politicians of his day who lobbied for grand, ornate portals. He'd had to battle such embroiderers, such meddlers, from the beginning. No one, it seems, wholeheartedly loves a simple thing. No one can resist trying to improve on it.

Two men approached on the path, laboriously pushing a baby stroller past a pair of ginkgo trees. The baby was immobilized in a snowsuit, its arms sticking out like a stuffed bear's; a wrapped box had been balanced on its puffy lap. A heavily made-up woman walked a dog sporting a wilted red bow. "All alone?" she whispered. "Want to come home with me?" I moved past her quickly. In the Ramble the paths were largely unmarked by footprints, the understory shrouded, the larger trees outlined with thick brushstrokes of snow. Disoriented, I walked from place to place, trying to remember how everything had looked two days ago, suddenly afraid that I might never see it all disrobed again. But why should I think that? Gradually the map reassembled itself in my mind. I found a bench nearby and brushed it off with my hand, then sat and lifted my face to the weak sun. How good it felt to be out in the air, to see no human being, no smokestack, car, or bus. One could imagine that the air was actually clean. I began to dream about the coming of spring, about how safe and warm the branches now were in their sleeves of snow, the inner life protected until it was time to press forth again. First, in mid-March, would come the red maple, the herald, followed by the American elm and the cornelian cherry. In early April the colors would arrive: forsythia and magnolia, spicebush and periwinkle, yellowroot and trout lily. In the second week of April, there would be Virginia bluebell, blue violet, Norway maple, dandelion.

I'd known these names and others like them long before I could recognize the plants they referred to. They were in the appendix of a book on Central Park that I found in my school library the fall after my mother and I had returned from the Adirondacks. At the time I hardly knew the park, even though our townhouse was only footsteps away from it. My experience of it was limited to the playground one maid or another had taken me to when I was younger and the sunken transverses on which I was occasionally whisked by taxi to destinations on the West Side. Well-behaved fourteen-year-olds did not spend time in the park, not in the early 1970s. But back in the city that fall, Henry-less, Central Park magnetized me. I studied the maps in the book with fascination: all that open land full of ponds and streams, woodland, rock formations, terraces, bridle paths, and bridges. My finger traced winding routes: I wanted to visit these places with enticing names such as Sheep Meadow, Bow Bridge, Turtle Pond, the Ramble, the Great Hill, and Duck Island. I read of the heroic efforts to earmark the land for public use, of the way the landscape was brought into being with hundreds of tons of dynamite that cleared millions of cubic yards of stone and dirt. When Frederick Olmsted came to check on his three thousand workers he stood knee-deep in stinking swampland that until recently had housed pigsties and slaughterhouses or been used as burial grounds for paupers. Goats left behind by squatters rambled over the rocks, nibbling bare the few trees that were able to grow.

I slipped away in the afternoons, telling the maid I was visiting a classmate. I walked in the park, ignoring the drunks and the dealers, learning the paths. I bought a field guide and began to identify trees and bushes. And I put my discoveries into the letters I wrote to Henry.

After the incident at the pond, Henry avoided me, but when his mother found out I was sick she sent him over with a tattered old botany book that she had found in the attic and some leaf samples. He laid the samples on my bedcovers and reminded me what each one was. I was still feverish, and everything I looked at was tinged with yellow. The leaves were drying out and left cracked bits on the covers. Henry seemed anxious, eager to please, and I knew that he had not wanted to stay away, had only thought that he was banished. I was so ill that I did not have the strength to tell him to go, and I found that I no longer wanted to.

Henry paged through the photographs. "The rhododendron," he said, trying to get my attention. "You have rhododendron behind your kitchen."

I looked at the picture he was pointing to. Did we have something in the yard that looked like that? I couldn't remember. It wasn't just that I was sick. I'd only begun to really look at bushes and flowers. Henry had taught me some of the names of trees, but I often mixed them up and had to be reminded. When lunchtime came and my mother did not appear Henry found a can of Campbell's tomato soup in the cupboard. He brought it to me, steaming in the bowl. I took one look at the oily orangey-red liquid and turned away, revolted.

"Give it a chance," said Henry. He picked up the spoon, filled it halfway, held it to my lips. I swallowed and the warmth spread through my chest, nosed down into my belly. I opened my mouth again, swallowed again. Once more. Then I had had enough. I turned my head away and fell asleep. When I awoke Henry was gone but the botany book was still there and my head felt clear. I opened at random to the chapter on taxonomy. "Man's impulse to name and classify must be nearly as old as his impulse toward food and warmth and companionship." I turned the pages with growing interest as the book explained that the angiosperms, or flowering plants, were separated into two groups, the dicots and the monocots, and that each of these was divided into half a dozen subgroups, or orders, which were in turn divided into families, and so on and so on until one arrived at the precise classification, the snug exact location, of a daisy or clover leaf or cattail. I have to tell Henry, I thought. Every plant—*everything*, I was suddenly sure—was related, everything was part of some larger group, some bigger whole. I had managed to get my socks and shirt on when the room began to spin and I fell to all fours on the floor.

I grew worse again, then better. One day I sat up in bed and drew primitive pictures and wrote out captions beneath them: DIVISION: Magnoliophyta. CLASS: Magnoliopsida. ORDER: Rosales. FAMILY: Rosaceae, the rose family. GENUS: *Malus*, the melons. SPECIES: *Malus pumila*. And there, red and plump, was my drawing of an apple.

By early August I had recovered but I invented lingering symptoms, complained of headaches, dizziness, strange pains. Henry, unsuspecting, still came to visit for a couple of hours every day. He came in smelling of the outdoors, of the pond and the ravine. We looked at the botany book, studied his beetles, and told jokes. Occasionally he glanced out of the window at the afternoon sun slanting over the yard and failed to suppress a sigh. I knew that he wanted to be out, knew that I was keeping him from pleasures. But I couldn't help it. I was afraid now: of air and wind and water, of the woods, of running and swimming, of Henry. And although nobody forced him to do so, Henry continued to come. He wanted a friend, and I was all he had that summer.

As September approached I began to dread Henry's return to the Westchester suburb where his family lived. "Can you visit me in the city?" I pleaded. "Can we be pen pals?" Sure, he told me. I wrote to him as soon as I arrived home, a long letter full of information about a science fair project I was planning. I felt freer on the page than in person; I wrote, "To my best friend" and signed off, "Love, Jack." I felt happy as I mailed the letter. Within hours I had written another one. Every day I wrote to Henry, but a week went by and I did not receive a letter in return. I was puzzled, then impatient, then, after another week went by, hurt. I reminded him of walks we had taken, things we had talked about. I detailed the facts I was learning about Central Park, the places there I had explored. Still there was no answer. During math and English class I scripted conversations with Henry, demanded reasons. I imagined riding the train to his town, finding my way to his house. I wrote, "I thought we were friends." I wrote, "You've broken my heart." I ripped these letters up, sure that by the next day something would arrive from Henry, chipper and good-hearted and with an explanation of his silence. Finally I wrote a letter full of other kinds of words. Chiefly I remember this sentence: "You deserve to die." And then, instead of destroying this letter too, I walked it out to the box on the corner and mailed it.

The first week of September the goldenrod would flower, and the white wood aster. After that the park would be dormant. Then, eventually, there would be spring again, the return of the red maples. I rose from my bench, threaded my way slowly back toward the city. The streets were filled now with traffic, although the day still had its comfortable holiday slackness. People greeted strangers, stopped to chat with doormen and dog walkers. The cars and buses passed almost apologetically.

The moment I opened the door to my apartment I knew that someone had been inside. There was a slight disturbance in the air, a sense of things subtly displaced. A copy of Locke's *Essay Concerning Human Understanding* lay on the side table cover up instead of cover down, as I was sure I'd left it. The sofa cushions had been plumped up, as if to disguise the fact that they'd been used. I could almost feel the pressure of footsteps on the thin nap of the carpet. On the mantelpiece, in place of Patrick's camera, was a sheet torn out of a pocket-sized notebook and held down by the shard of glass Patrick had taken the previous day from his shoe.

Please forgive. I'd hoped to find you in.

—Patrick

I'd hoped to find you in. I read this brief note, scrawled in hurried, uneven, rather childish handwriting, several times over, parsing the implications of "Please forgive." Did those words, placed first, rob "I'd hoped to find you in" of any intimacy? Had Patrick only meant to say that if I'd been home he wouldn't have needed to come in without my permission? But in that case he might as easily have written, "Please forgive the intrusion."

I'd hoped to find you in. I thought of the master key in his pocket, the key to my rooms, the power he had to enter any time he wanted, and it gave me an uneasy thrill. I left the note by the shard of glass and the business card and hurried into the bedroom. I spread my palm on the bedcovers, touched the shade of the reading lamp. No vibration of him here. In the kitchen, though, he was back. I stared at a glass, conjured Patrick's long fingers wrapped around it, holding it up to the bulb. I saw him opening cabinets and peering inside at the cereal boxes, Domino sugar, graham crackers, dented cans of food from my uncle's time.

It was Christmas Day and Patrick was not out of town. He was not too busy with family visits or parties or a sweetheart to have come here, expecting to see me. He had been spending the day by himself. He'd been lonely. He'd thought . . .

He'd thought nothing. He'd needed his camera. His family had been sitting around the fireplace, waiting to be photographed, and he'd realized that he did not have his camera. I'll run over there, he told them. It's just around the corner.

Was Patrick just around the corner?

I spied the spiral notebook I had used on my research trips to the law library and picked it up, leafed through my notes. *Adverse possession. Rationale of rent control.* These words and phrases were soothing. I thought of turning on the oven, then considered the heating bill and instead pulled the quilt off my bed and wrapped it tightly around myself. I read for hours, the words on the page taking on a strange sheen, a pulsation that was somehow permeated with Patrick's lean form, his stoop, the loopy script on the note he'd left me.

The days passed, and Patrick did not come. No one came. No one cleaned away the debris from the fire or scoured away the smell. A fine silty ash wafted down from the top floor and coated the stairwell, fingered under my door and into the fibers of my carpet. I took a sponge to the walls but that only spread a gray watery stain. The broken windows upstairs sent down whining swells of cold air.

One evening just before the New Year I paused at my front door with my key in the lock, sensing a greater absence than usual above me. Upstairs I found Mrs. Fiore's door gaping open upon bare walls, her rust-colored carpet littered with plastic tree branches. Gone were the wall mirror, the photographs, the pots and pans. That night I was more aware than before of the silence of the building after dark. Only now did I recall the sounds that used to be there when I'd believed there were no sounds at all: Mr. Flax's phlegmy cough, the raised voices of the Porters arguing, the ringing of phones.

New Year's Day arrived. I visited the park and at day's end stood on the bridge looking out over Brooklyn. Tiny figures moved on the promenade, celebrants in the cold. When it was time to return home I slid my MetroCard, stripe facing left, into the turnstile at Broadway-Nassau, and a digital display flashed out that I had two rides remaining. I saw neither the man with the flat briefcase nor the woman with the purse. But the advertisement-lined platform and the whoosh of the arriving train and the jolt and tremble of the car were all familiar, and as I tucked the subway card back into my wallet I felt that I would get used to this new way of doing things.

Another evening, having found my way downtown a bit too early, I took a slight detour along Fourth Avenue, thinking to see if any of the secondhand bookstores from my student days still existed. After some circling about I was delighted to find one I remembered, the metal cart outside its door still filled with fifty-cent paperbacks. Long ago, before my time, dozens of secondhand bookstores had stretched north from the Village along Fourth Avenue, this one specializing in music, that one in art books or international fiction. They had constituted a city within a city, a subculture with its own hangers-on and celebrities. In histories of the neighborhood I read about the owner who could recite verbatim from any page of *Paradise Lost*, another rumored to be a former lover of W. H. Auden's. When the noise of my classes or dormitory became too much I would spend an evening exploring the stores that remained, seeking out the smell or atmosphere I craved most. Leaning against the shelves or flopped in a chair, I'd read poetry and philosophy and history, cookbooks and old gun catalogues, Boy Scout pamphlets and economics textbooks, only dimly aware of the occasional cough or shuffle of feet.

Peterson's, the bookstore I now stood before was called, a good plain name. I went inside. Yes, I remembered it: the owner took an interest in regional literature, the history of New York State and of Manhattan, the area's flora and fauna and waterways. There were old maps on the wall, time-darkened paintings of Colonial figures. Near the front door two men were bent over an enormous map dotted with what looked like checkers. One set of checkers bore the American flag, the other a swastika. I gravitated toward a shelf filled with books on native plants. I had been reading only a short while when a man emerged from the rear of the store and asked me to leave. I looked at him in surprise, my mind still full of the characteristics of *E. americanus*, the strawberry bush. "What for?" I asked. He was tall and thin-cheeked and wore a faded plaid shirt. Mr. Peterson, presumably.

"I don't need to tell you what for," he said. "This is my store and I don't want you here."

I glanced at myself to see if what I was wearing was torn or stained, if anything about me was offensive. Maybe he was joking with me. I smiled nervously and reached for another book.

"Did you hear him or what?"

One of the war-gamers stood up, his belly spilling over his belt. He shook out his long coarse hair.

"I haven't done anything," I murmured. The room had developed a sinister aspect: the low ceiling, the dim lights, the big-bellied man in front of me and the wraith like Mr. Peterson behind.

"Haven't done anything?" jeered the big-bellied man. He stepped toward me, his heavy boots thudding against the floor.

When I saw that he did not mean to stop, my stomach lurched and I sprinted around him, the book tumbling from my fingers. I careered onto the first side street I saw, turned and turned again, jogging crazily until I spotted the lighted globes of a subway. *There must be some mistake*, I thought. *They have me confused with somebody else.* Just before reaching the subway entrance I caught sight of my reflection in a lighted window filled with medical supplies: prosthetics, elastic bandages, bedpans. The bizarre display stopped me and I paused, panting, resting my forehead against the glass. When I raised my head again, still breathing heavily, I did look, reflected to myself, like someone criminal, or at least disorderly and subnormal. I leaned in, trying to see deeper into my reflection, but my image dissolved as I grew closer. I bared my teeth, caught the flash of white. Then I hobbled down into the subway and rode home with my eyes closed.

The weather grew bitter. For several days in mid-January I cut short my visits to the park and on one of these days I took shelter in a small art gallery on the Upper West Side so that I could thaw my numbed fingers. A sleepy-looking woman asked if I would like a mug of hot tea while I looked around. I very rarely went to museums or galleries, but I found myself drawn to some paintings done in broad washes of reds and yellows on large irregular ovals of paper. It occurred to me that these were paintings my mother might have liked. "Please sign our guest book," the woman said, handing me the tea. At the top of the page for that day I wrote: *John Frederick Ronan*. In another corner of the room a different artist had filled an entire canvas with black dots. I looked more closely. Some of the dots were a bit larger and some were smaller, but they all marched in long, closely spaced lines that looped and crossed and sometimes sent off shoots in new directions. There must have been tens of thousands of these little dots; the canvas looked like a hiking map with trails running wild. I thought of the artist bending over his brush, patiently dabbing in circle after circle, repetition after repetition, his back aching, his eyes beginning to swim. The image oppressed me. I turned away from the canvas and asked where I should put my mug. "Come again, Mr. Ronan," the woman called after me.

Where was Patrick? The weeks passed. Why had he not returned? "Please forgive," said the note on my mantelpiece. "I'd hoped to find you in." The pressure of his pen on the flimsy paper, the childish uncontrol of the handwriting, the torn bit at the top where he had removed the paper from the pad: these were all so physical to me, so palpable. It was as if he were there in the room with me. Yet he did not come. I tried to picture what parts of the city he was working in each day, calculated the possibility of running into him on the street. Less likely, I thought, than the possibility of spotting a set of identical twins. Gradually I came to berate myself for having looked for hints and invitations in a tossed-off note. More than once I determined to throw the note away, but it would have felt like disposing of a living thing.

In the middle of one night I woke to hear the hiss of steam in the radiators. I sighed and turned over in bed, kicking off layers. In the morning I learned why the heat had returned. As I was shaving, I heard the slam of the downstairs door, followed by the sound of footsteps and of men coughing. Soon a radio was turned on. Spanish lyrics floated toward me as I opened my front door. A latecomer passed, dressed in workman's whites, and looked at me with surprise.

"You live here?" he asked.

I said that I did. He scratched his nose. "Mr. Giglio said nobody is living in the building. There was a fire, no?"

"Yes, a fire," I agreed. "But I still live here."

I walked through my rooms touching the mantelpiece, the counters, the tables: surfaces that had been cave-cold for weeks and now were warm again. The oily, unfamiliar scent of the heat made me sleepy and lazy. I could not seem to get myself out of doors. I made myself some toast and delighted in the way the air-softened butter spread creamily over my toast instead of lying in stubborn hard slivers. I scrambled an egg just to prolong the meal. Then I drew a hot bath and lay in it, listening to the scraping and talking of the workers upstairs.

When the buzzer rang I was frightened for a moment; I had forgotten what the sound meant. But immediately afterward I conjured up Patrick's face. I stepped out of the bath and dried myself quickly, threw on pants and a shirt. As I hurried down the stairs I told myself to be reasonable: it was just one of the workers, someone had gotten locked out. At the bottom of the staircase I made out a short man composed of blurred shifting shapes behind the smoked glass of the vestibule door. Raising his voice to be heard he told me that he needed my signature. I unlocked the door and the man handed me some papers: CIVIL COURT OF THE CITY OF NEW YORK. I read them quickly, hoping to spy some technical error that would allow me to hand them back and tell the man to come back another time. Perhaps my name would be misspelled, or the wrong apartment number listed. "PLEASE TAKE NOTICE that a hearing at which you must appear will be held at the Civil Court of the City of New York. . . . PLEASE TAKE NOTICE that if you fail to establish any defense to the allegations of this petition. . . . PLEASE TAKE NOTICE that in the event of your failure to answer and appear . . ."

I held the papers in one hand, the pen the man had given me in the other. "If you would please," urged the man. I signed the papers, and he disappeared. It struck me that I had no one to tell the news. I gazed at the dirty snow banked motionless across the street. In front of one of the brownstones sat a man shrouded in a garbage bag, another scrap of bag tied like a kerchief around his head. Impossible that I'd never noticed him before. I stepped onto the street to take a walk, clear my head, but before I had been gone a few minutes I realized that I had no coat on. I circled back, banging on the front door until one of the workmen let me in.

That day and the next and the next I spent extra time at the law library filling my head with facts, precedents, obscure lines of reasoning. I read case after case, scribbled notes and arguments until my eyes burned. I walked up and down the library stacks on the off chance that the right book, the book that would save me, would jump out and announce the perfect answer. Did fifteen years' residence entitle me to any kind of rights? Would anybody say in hard print that it was so?

On the fourth evening, my energies flagging, I returned home before dusk to hear women's voices and the sound of vacuuming. An astringent odor met me in the vestibule, a mixture of lemon and ammonia. I went up the newly swept stairs. A woman outside the Porters' door held a mop in one hand and a cigarette in the other. Smoke curled around me as I continued up to the second landing.

"Mr. Gorse?" I knew the voice instantly, though it took me a moment to realize that it was speaking to me. Gorse was the name I used at the bank, a name linked in my mind with my monthly stipend, with paperwork. I wondered if

Patrick thought it as ugly a name as I did. Gorse: a bush with thorns. Even my mother had refused it, keeping her maiden name for the stage. Grace Gorse for an actress? An abomination.

He called down from Mrs. Fiore's floor, saying that he'd brought me something. He asked me to wait, he would be right down. I stood where I was, a patient child, straining to hear what he was saying to one of the workmen. In a moment the man came clomping down the stairs, his tool belt rattling, and passed on. Patrick followed, shrugging off his knapsack. He tugged at some cords and pulled out of the knapsack's mouth a flat gray envelope.

"Please," I said. "Call me Jack."

Patrick handed the envelope to me. I lifted the flap and drew out a large photograph of a man standing in my kitchen. Was this me? The man's eyes were unfocused, his face slack. There was stubble on his chin; his bathrobe was lumpy and shabby. For a moment I was too surprised to speak.

Patrick bent over the photograph and began to use a vocabulary I couldn't follow: *depth of field*, *cropping*, *burning-in*. He seemed to be very interested in this technical conversation, or, more accurately, lecture, but I was preoccupied with the age of the man in the picture. His forehead was high and bald and his hair stood up in thinning tufts at the crown. The lower half of the face was not as square and firm as I was sure it ought to be. The shoulders slumped and the bathrobe looked old-fashioned in some way I could not have defined.

"It's for you," Patrick told me. Was he really not aware of how pathetic the man in the picture looked? Patrick's eyes urged the gift on me; he clearly wished me to be pleased. I studied the photograph again, searching for whatever it was that had caused Patrick to feel I looked "interesting." Failing to find it, I pasted a smile onto my face and tried to appear flattered. I think I thanked him. All of a sudden I had an overwhelming desire to tell him about the eviction papers. I reached out to steady myself on the banister, to fend off my shyness while I gathered the right words in my mouth.

Patrick's cell phone rang. He apologized and turned away as people do when they speak into a phone. My throat was dry and I stared yet again at the photograph. *Horrible*, I thought. Patrick was saying something about crown molding. I realized that when he turned back to me there would be no graceful way to begin, no way to speak of the eviction papers or the photograph or even the weather. I simply did not have the words. The vacuuming started up again on the floor below, filling the stairwell with white noise. I did not want Patrick to turn, pushing the phone into his pocket, and see my speechlessness and trembling. While the roar of cleaning covered the sound of my steps, I slipped away.

Eleven

Some nights I dream about the Down twins. They sit on the library steps in their ironed white shirts, their neat school blazers, shivering anxiously in the wind, yet never doubting that someone is coming to take them home. I see their almond eyes, their broad faces. The wind blows their hair into strange and wild shapes. Or I dream I walk out of my apartment, away from the boarded-up fireplace, the couch, all my books, and follow Patrick down long dark Manhattan streets terrifying in their unfamiliarity. When I wake I catch my breath, remembering where I am, that I do not own my bed, my room, the hours of my day. I remember that in the night one of my roommates shouted out. What was his dream? In a moment I will have to get up, wash my face, and walk into the darkness of the abbey. But for a few seconds longer I can pretend that I am still sovereign and free. I think of Central Park and what is blooming there now: columbine and Solomon's seal, Photinia, buttercup. Soon there will also be roses, mountain laurel, catalpa.

I wait while the other men use the bathroom, and turn my back to the room to dress. I brush my teeth and glance at myself in the mirror, always surprised to find myself really here, in these rooms, this place. The last out the door, I provoke scowls as I rush moments late into the meditation hall. I avoid looking at the abbot, who has told Joku that I cannot stay on as a gardener and must make other arrangements within the month.

During *zazen* I think about something I read in the library the other day, that the Sanskrit word for *monk* comes from another word that means *to beg*. I picture the monks of tradition walking the countryside with their begging bowls in hand, peasants beckoning them in to feed them meat and fish and tea. There were strict rules against monks' keeping any food from one day to the next; each day they were required to start again with nothing. How good, I thought, to know that one's bowl would be filled over and over. How good that its emptiness would be prescribed, a thing without shame.

After *zazen* the abbot always gives a brief lecture. Today it is about remorse. Suppose you have injured somebody, he says. You have lied or cheated, abused someone emotionally or physically. Afterward you feel guilty, or would like to. But Buddhism prescribes action, not feeling. For the Buddhist, the abbot reminds us, feeling is merely an indulgence. We should not waste time feeling guilty. Rather, we should make amends to those we have injured.

We rise and crowd into the dining hall for breakfast. I can't help thinking what I always think: It is I who am due amends. I catch Joku watching me as, heads bowed, we repeat the chant before consuming a meal. *Seventy-two labors brought us this food; we should know how it comes to us.* I have never been able to shake the feeling that he can read my thoughts. I stop him as he passes with his tray, and tell him that I have news.

On my last visit to the nursery in Conklin, I explain, I noticed a Help Wanted sign; the owner, Mr. Endicott, was looking for someone to work Saturdays loading customers' cars with heavy bags of peat and dirt. I told him that I was interested in the job. As I recount the incident to Joku, I remember the way that Mr. Endicott looked me up and down, replying with New England terseness that he hoped I was strong enough. I was, I promised. I did not bother to think about how I would get to work, or whether the abbot would give me permission to go.

"Whatever I earn I'll give back to the abbey," I tell Joku. I point out that with the employee discount I'll get, the abbey's supplies will cost less. I insist that this is a start.

Joku looks embarrassed. Panicked, I start to make predictions: Mr. Endicott will give me another day of work before long; by fall I could be with him full-time. I just need a little more time to get on my feet. And the bonsai—what will happen to the bonsai if I leave? Finally I find myself blurting out that I have some money in a bank account in Manhattan, it's been tied up with red tape, but within days

I should have access to it. I can make up the difference between my pay at Endicott's and the monthly resident's fee. A bit of paperwork and it will be taken care of.

Joku takes a gulp of coffee. Meals are quick here; no sooner do we sit down than it is time to clear the tables for morning chores. Conversations have to be quick, too. "It's not just about the money," he says. He says that I've shown no evidence of interest in Buddhism as a way of life. The abbey is not a boardinghouse. He will speak to the abbot, but he warns me not to be optimistic. He suggests that I contact one of the social service groups in Burlington.

People are getting up and busing their trays. Joku slides a brochure from a rubber-banded stack and hands it to me. "Open it," he says. I do and on the second panel I see the two of us, a monk with wire-rimmed glasses and a man with thinning hair and a sweatshirt, caught in the middle of a conversation. The man holds a book—you can just make out the title, *The Psychopathology of Everyday Life*. A ripple of fear goes through me. "May I keep this?" I ask. "Certainly," Joku says, standing up. "I've got hundreds more."

When I return to my room later I surprise one of my roommates by speaking to him and asking for an envelope and a stamp. I carefully tear out the picture of Joku and me and put it into the envelope. On the front of the envelope I write out the address of Patrick's office in New York City. My heart races, filled with a strange excitement. Then I walk the letter down to the secretary's desk and place it in the tray for outgoing mail.

Twelve

I propped the photograph Patrick had given me on the mantelpiece next to his business card and his note and the broken glass, and over the days it ceased to disturb me so much. The homeliness of the man in the picture became unsurprising, like the homeliness of a familiar piece of furniture. I got used to this face, its paralyzed uncertainty, the bewildered mouth. I saved the gray envelope the photo had come in and put it on the mantelpiece as well. It had once been addressed to someone else, a Mr. Michael Taylor on West Forty-Second Street, but a thick black line had been drawn through the typed name and above it was scrawled "Jack Gorse." Seeing the name in Patrick's handwriting, I could almost develop an affection for it. I traced the letters with my finger, feeling my hand merged with Patrick's as we made the long slash of the *J*, the swollen loop of the *G*. I wondered when Patrick would next descend like the

intermittent angel he was, bearing a gift or leaving some
sign of himself behind. Each evening on my return home
I listened in the hopes of hearing his voice calling down to
me from above, and when I didn't hear it I was sure that at
another time, and soon, I would.

In the mornings I combed my hair carefully and touched
my neck and wrists with some drugstore cologne. On impulse I visited a large, fluorescent-lit discount clothing store
near Union Square. I became anxious when I saw all the
circular racks topped by big signs marked with prices and
exclamation points, but before I could retreat a salesman
seized my shoulders and asked me my size. He pulled a
shirt with blue stripes from a rack and held it up to me. I
imagined wearing the fresh new shirt the next time Patrick
saw me, and I let the salesman lead me over to the register.
There I handed over more bills than I had paid at once for
anything in a very long time.

Patrick did not come. One evening as I entered the building I heard Giglio's voice amid the softer tones of the workmen and I darted into my apartment with a sense that it was
wiser to conceal myself. Then I was ashamed and walked
about the apartment noisily, opening cabinets and turning
the sink on and off, to prove I was not afraid of my landlord.
Most nights the building was silent when I returned, and I
would linger on the ground floor to track the progress of
the work being done there. Amid the drywall and pieces of
pipe and coiled wire, beauties, as Patrick had hoped, were
being revealed. The workmen's painstaking demolition had

revealed an extra row of molding in the front room and an ornamental keystone on the fireplace. A brand-new chandelier with curving arms sat in a corner, waiting for a chance to illuminate the refurbished interior. When I saw these things my confidence failed me and I vowed to spend more time at the law library. Once there, I doodled heavyheartedly on the pages of my notebook and pictured boarding a bus to Pennsylvania, knocking on the doors of relatives of my mother's who had never met me and had probably never even heard of me. The aunt who called me after my uncle's death was herself long gone. I pictured some matron, a woman with grown children, idle and dissatisfied in late middle age, taking me in. She would give me a room—wouldn't there have to be a well-swept attic room with floral curtains on the windows?—and allow me to live there, a harmless eccentric, turning the pages of my books and going for my little walks. I would be the man that every modest-sized town possesses, the one in the shabby cardigan who pushes the grocery cart home from two miles away, shambling down the busy commercial road, returning four times a week for his two containers of yogurt, quart of milk, and favorite brand of crackers.

Each evening when I got home I looked for the note that would be propped on the mantelpiece next to my photograph:

> *I stopped by to say hello.*
> *I've been meaning to come see you but I could not*

leave the office.
I've been meaning to come see you but I was sick.
I was in an accident.
I was too shy.

As the days went by and no note appeared I thought that perhaps Patrick was waiting for me to get in touch with him. He had given me a gift—might it be my move? Patrick *was* shy. The photograph was his way of reaching out. What was he reaching out for? What did I want him to be reaching for? I didn't dwell on these questions. I only thought about the thrill of what he'd said to me—that he found me "interesting." But I could not imagine dialing the number on the business card. What if he were put off by my forwardness?

When the day arrived for me to appear in court I woke at the same hour as always, yet as soon as I opened my eyes I had the sense that I was already hopelessly behind schedule. I was not due in court until one, but I skipped breakfast and straightaway put on my new shirt, an old suit jacket, and a tie. From my nightstand I removed my notebook of legal research. I looked it over one more time and then pushed it aside. My research was pointless. I had no case—I'd never had a case. What good were my notes on the woman whose fiancé had died before she could move into his rent-controlled apartment? What did her story have to do with me? My notebook was filled with such case histories, as useless as fragments of fairy tales. In a different state of mind I might have been able to take these fragments and weave a clever argument, forge analogies. Hadn't I been trained as a lawyer? But I had no heart for cleverness today. It all seemed like lies, lies and evasions. I had no argument.

When I entered his store earlier than usual Carl looked up at me in mild surprise but said nothing. He watched as I went to the shelf and returned with the book I wanted.

"No time to stay today," I said. "I'll just take this."

Carl received the small blue volume from my hands, licked his finger, and turned one page after another. Finally he set the book down, and with his lean old-man's fingers, white hair springing from the knuckles, he punched the price into a battered adding machine. The machine whirred and spat some numbers onto a receipt which he tore off and saved for himself. "Three seventy-five," he told me.

It occurred to me that I might be making a mistake. There would always be a gap now on the shelf between Wallace Stevens and William Butler Yeats. Worse, one day some other book would come to fill that gap, and it would be as if this book had never existed. But I paid my money and left. *This poet is very dear to me*, I would say, when I handed the book to Patrick. *He has been my companion for a long time. Do get past the unfamiliar diction, the excessive formality. You will be rewarded.*

Hungry now, I stopped for a fried egg and toast at the Stardust Diner. Marion blinked at me quizzically and glanced at the clock over the front counter. When I left the tip she scooped it up suspiciously.

I walked on. At the New York Public Library I let my gaze pass momentarily through the ornate doors to poke and pry among the thousands of shelves of books within, and I felt an unexpected trickle of hope. You do have an argument, I told myself. Perhaps not an argument a judge can understand, but a true and good one all the same, an argument housed in all those books in there. In one, Aristotle says that the best life is not a life of politics or of making or doing of any kind. He says that making and doing are good and useful, but that the real purpose of houses and pots and bread is to free our minds for contemplation, the one task they are really designed for.

I walked on again, snatching at the possibilities, beginning to construct a judge who was listening to this brand-new reasoning. He was a wiry, noble-looking man in his sixties or seventies, with glasses that he took off and put on as my points particularly struck him.

Your Honor, I said respectfully, *I recognize that I have no legal claim to this apartment. But isn't it possible that I have a moral claim? John Locke wrote that no man is made for the use of another. Confucius said the same, long before Locke: a gentleman is not an implement.*

No. I stopped short at a corner and a homeless man, thinking I was stopping to give him some change, said, "Thank you, sir." I looked down at him and his cardboard sign, and I fished out a quarter to drop into his plastic container.

No, I had started where I ought to end up. I had to lead the judge to this conclusion. I must begin differently.

Your Honor, Locke wrote that what gives a man a right to property is that he has mixed his labor with that property. Hegel added that when a man exercises his will upon a thing, he makes that thing a part of himself.

Your Honor, I have spent thousands and thousands of hours within the walls of my apartment, reading and thinking. Those walls, the furniture, even my carpets, have absorbed my most sincere and relentless labor. My labors have been not with hammer and nails but with the tools of analysis, inference, reason. I am a solitary soul, unfit for traditional work. Is it so wrong, so inconceivable, that one in a hundred or one in a thousand men should be like me, should be allowed the leisure to pursue higher things? Some people inherit such leisure, but I have not. I am not a drunk or a social menace. I work; it is just that my work does not make or do.

I suppose you will say, Your Honor, that I should find other ways to support my habit of reading. I should write articles or teach. As for teaching, please remember that I find it almost unbearable to be in the company of other people. As for writing, I have never wished to reduce the complexity and uniqueness of the great thinkers to pale summaries. In the time it would take me to write one insignificant article I could read half a dozen truly valuable books. Should only geniuses, only people who offer a verifiable brilliance to the world, be allowed a life among books? Thoreau said that it would please him to imagine a government that could tolerate the existence of a few men who wished to live aloof from it, "not meddling with it, nor embraced by it."

I walked through Midtown, past Union Square, blind to everything around me, refining my words in an attempt to fashion the right mix of wise self-assertion and deference to the court, but when I reached the broad expanse of the Bowery I finally slowed my steps and looked around. Trucks idled beside the old four-story tenements; a man hurried by in a grease-stained jumpsuit. Something about this neighborhood, still untouched by improvement, always riveted me. You could glimpse the taproot of the city here, Manhattan's origins in industry and manual labor. Nearly everything I could identify in the shop windows or open-air lots was either heavy or dirty: auto parts, pianos, restaurant vats, steel cable, newspapers, gasoline. There were mechanics' garages and places to rent U-Hauls. I had the sense that this neighborhood would soon slip into the past just like the others, that in fifteen years it would be filled with gleaming office buildings and chic restaurants. But for now it remained unassimilated. The only other part of Manhattan that so fully gave me this illusion of suspended time was Central Park. Whenever I ran my hand over the bark of old trees and looked out onto marshy lakes and open meadows that had remained nearly unaltered for a hundred and fifty years, I could feel that in season after season the land continued to be saved from the future and for the future.

I moved on again, and the street signs and shop signs gradually acquired a subscript of Chinese characters as the neighborhood of the old working class blended into the neighborhood of the new one. I resumed my composing.

Your Honor, I see myself as one link in a chain reaching back even beyond Aristotle, to the beginning of cognition and contemplation, one link that makes it just a bit more likely that the chain will remain intact. I liked Chinatown. I was fond of the glass-fronted photographers' shops, the secretive cultural associations, the bakeries and jewelers, the sharp odors of root vegetables and leather. I stopped at a bakery and bought myself two almond cookies and a cup of strong tea. How to wrap up my peroration? Now the civic buildings began to appear. I passed the main criminal courthouse and up ahead I spotted the address to which I was headed. *Your Honor, let me ask you this: Does the world need four more high-priced Manhattan rentals? Or do the immortals need one more true reader? Yes, they do. They desperately do. Somebody must keep their books and thoughts alive.*

Finally I arrived at my destination. A metal barricade on one side of the building gave the impression that trouble was expected. I passed a metal detector and stood with my arms outspread while a plump woman passed a silver rod up and over my body. The rod never touched me, yet the woman's actions felt intimate, unclean. When I entered the room on the third floor where the trial was to take place, I saw that Paul Giglio and his lawyer were already seated in the spectator benches. There was another trial in session, and in order to quell my nervousness I watched the stenographer, a turbaned man sitting at the front of the room. Eventually I raised my eyes to the judge, who looked nothing like the judge I had been mentally lecturing. She was petite and Asian and wore deep-red lipstick and large silver earrings shaped like crescent moons. Her small hands darted in and out of her robes and I observed the impatient curl of her mouth as she listened to the defendant speak.

An hour and a half later, I walked out of the courthouse lobby and onto Centre Street, where I caught a whiff of river water. I turned and followed that scent as if it would save me. *I must get to the bridge,* I thought; *there I'll be able to think.* To Giglio's lawyer's questions I had replied with a simple yes or no. The most difficult was the first. Is your name John Frederick Ronan Gorse? Yes, I said quietly. Was John Frederick Ronan your uncle? Yes. Did he pass away in March of 1984? Yes. Did you move into Apartment Two at that time? Yes. I observed Judge Marjorie Ng's busy hands and fringe of bangs. "Mr. Gorse, do you have any questions for Mr. Giglio?" she asked. I stood up clumsily. Judge Ng was waiting, I thought, to hear something that would surprise her, something that would reveal this case to be more complicated than it seemed.

"Your Honor," I began. My voice shook. "Please don't take my apartment away. I can't survive if you do. Thank you."

I collapsed into my seat and the judge looked at me in dismay. "Thank you, Mr. Gorse," she said finally. She called for a ten-minute adjournment, grabbing a disorderly stack of papers as she went. Giglio stood and stretched. The turbaned stenographer unscrewed a bottle of Evian and drank avidly.

When the judge returned she announced that I had ten days to remove myself and my belongings from the apartment owned by Paul X. Giglio Associates. Then she turned to her clerk and asked for the name of the next case.

The Brooklyn Bridge rose before me, its great harp strings waving in the white sky. I stepped onto the pedestrian ramp, feeling the heavy vibrations of the traffic beneath, and climbed toward the openness at the top, toward that feeling of suspension. A helicopter overhead silenced everything except the roaring in my ears. With every footstep I reviled myself. Aristotle on the best life! Hegel and Locke! Would the likes of Hegel and Locke ever have defended a man like me? A man who produced nothing, contributed nothing, perhaps understood nothing? The only argument I had been able to muster in the end, the only truth I had been able to speak, was this: *I want, I need.* Was that worthy of the greats? And was that all my life amounted to?

When I got to the New York tower I stopped and looked out toward the familiar sprawl of Brooklyn. Even on this dull winter day the East River was full of life, shooting up in white peaks and crashing against the pilings. There was a smell as of damp bread in the old stone. Lady Liberty poked out, a gray shadow, on her barely visible slip of island. Ahead lay the opposite shore, as far somehow as if it were another country, with houses and neighborhoods full of people busy and unknown, and beyond them, invisible to me, more water, and beyond that, more land, more people.

Where could I go? I did not continue out over the water but instead backed against the tower, sheltering myself from the crowds. A teenager loped by, an aggressive beat leaking from his earphones. I worried some loose threads on the book in my pocket. I would watch Patrick as he turned the fragile pages, listen as he read the poems aloud. *But it is so gloomy*, he would say, placing his finger on a page, appealing to me. *Yes*, I would answer.

I turned back down the footpath, made my way slowly to land. There is always, I thought, somewhere to go, if only for a few hours. I crossed the busy intersection at the foot of the bridge but instead of entering the Broadway-Nassau station I continued westward, to Fulton Street, and descended there. Commuters stood two deep in the stale air on the platform; the beginning of rush hour had already arrived. The ground shook with the departure of a train. Once I had stood in this station as a body was carried off a car. People had murmured contradictorily about a heart attack, a knifing, and I remembered now the stretcher, with the sheet pulled up and the man obscured beneath it. I stood back, against the wall, willing the train to come.

At Twenty-Third Street I pushed out of the crowded car and made my way past well-groomed townhouses and canopied greengrocers to the bare industrial stretches nearer to the Hudson, where the wind blew hard and cold down the unsheltered avenues. Just off Eleventh Avenue I found the squat, functional building where Patrick's firm was located. A name next to an entryway buzzer revealed that the company occupied the second floor. I stood gazing upward— Patrick might be only a dozen feet away from me right now, practically within reach of my outstretched arm. He might be sitting at a desk just above my head. I stood for a long time absorbing his presence but when I heard the elevator rumble toward the ground floor I took fright and exited the building without looking back.

People moved past me with their dogs and their groceries, dodging me and making sounds of annoyance, until I realized I had spent several minutes standing in the middle of the sidewalk. I began to ask passersby if they knew about a Buddhist center nearby, a place to meditate. Some people did not answer, others shrugged their ignorance, but after a while a woman wearing a colorful scarf stopped and gave me directions to the Chelsea Zen Center, three blocks away. I thanked her and hurried on.

The Chelsea Zen Center occupied a small storefront nestled unobtrusively between a shoe repair shop and a dentist's, so unobtrusively that at first I passed it and had to double back. The interior, furnished with upholstered sofas and a couple of low coffee tables, was as modest and casual as someone's living room. A young man at a folding table told me that the evening meditation session was about to begin. I made to follow some other latecomers, but he tapped on a goldfish bowl full of five- and ten-dollar bills and said that a donation would be appreciated. I rummaged in my pocket and came up with a wadded bill. The door to the meditation room was propped open; people were sitting silently on mats or chatting quietly. There were rows of shoes and purses and knapsacks outside the door. I looked into the room but did not see Patrick. A man in a robe carrying a tall stick quietly shut the door, and I heard from within the sound of a high, pure bell. As I left the center I thought about retrieving my money from the goldfish bowl but the young man was still there, looking vigilant.

The subway I rode home was unfamiliar, packed to the doors, overheated. When I arrived home, fumbling for my key, I discovered a neat round hole in the outer door where the lock cylinder ought to have been. Startled, I gave the door a push and it swung heavily open. The vestibule door too had a hole through its middle. I wondered how long it would take before street people and vandals made the same discovery I had.

Fortunately my own apartment was locked up just as I'd left it, my rooms still private and secure. I bolted the door from the inside, took a few deep breaths, and went to make myself a cup of coffee. When I had drunk enough of it to calm my nerves I made a second one and placed it on the kitchen table opposite me. I moved the chair over as if inviting a guest to join me. Then I set about making two ham-and-cheese sandwiches. I put the second sandwich next to the second coffee cup. I ate standing up, watching the other place setting, and when I brought my dishes to the sink I brought the other dishes there as well. I cleaned up and went into my bedroom to get a pillow. I laid it on the living room floor and, removing my shoes, seated myself upon it, attempting to get into a cross-legged position. The best I could muster was a froglike arrangement that left my ankles dragging awkwardly on the floor. I straightened my back and conjured up the sound of that beautiful bell. I imagined that I was Patrick, his long legs folded under him, his fingers gently clasped. I imagined the quiet in his mind, his slow, calm breathing.

Very early the next morning I returned to the Zen center, not knowing what time it opened, and stood reading the flyers taped to its door. Around nine-thirty a young woman with cropped hair and cat's-eye glasses opened up and I followed her in. She hung her coat in a closet and I wondered if I could manage to slip into that closet after the final meditation of the evening, emerging to sleep on one of the sofas until daybreak. I would be safe here, I thought, even comfortable. I could wake up each morning in time to join the first sessions. All day I would meditate and attend classes, and when Patrick arrived, I would already be here.

"Can I help you with something?" the woman asked, and when I could not remember what I needed help with she handed me a brochure. "Everything is in there," she said.

On a stoop across the street from the center I read the brochure and watched the door. Gradually people began to come and go. The back of the brochure described the Chelsea Zen Center's parent center in Vermont, a place called Infinite Light Abbey, and showed an abstract swirl or pattern. I stared at this for so long that I began to see the pattern hover about me in the air. The brochure spoke of the abbey's two-hundred-acre nature preserve in the Green Mountains, "an environment carefully constructed to promote study and introspection." I read the schedule of classes and events over and over again, uncertain which appealed to me. Should I register for Calligraphy? Tea Ceremony? Introduction to Zen?

My plan was simple. When Patrick arrived I would enter after him. I would sit at the back of the room, so as not to be seen, not to startle him, and I would watch and imitate his posture, his attitude of concentration. When the session was done I would go up to him and greet him. *I have been wanting to give you something*, I would say. I would take the book out of my pocket, press it into his hands, and speak my few words. *Do get past the unfamiliar diction, the excessive formality.* Then I would walk away, to show both him and myself that I did not intend to be a nuisance, that I only wished to issue an invitation.

The stream of people making their way to the center slowed. At eleven there was again a burst of activity for the calligraphy class, and at noon there was another meditation session. Despite having had nothing to eat all day, I did not leave my post. People went in and out of the building. I read and reread the brochure. Was Patrick more likely to take a pottery class or sign up for a lecture series? The third time that the policewoman making the rounds spotted me she gave me a probing look but passed on without speaking. The light faded and the air grew colder; the doors opened for the last meditation session of the day. At seven-fifteen, the woman with cropped hair locked up and left. I walked away, strangely buoyant. Patrick had not come today, but he would come another day. In the meantime I was near him, ready for him, sure of a glimpse before long. Computer screens in the darkened windows of townhouses exploded with fireworks of shapes and colors. I stopped at a coffee shop and ordered two hamburgers, two eggs, and two glasses of rice pudding. "My friend will be here shortly," I explained to the waitress, whose face I did not want to look at too closely, for it would not be the face of Marion. Later, after the waitress said it was too bad my friend hadn't shown up, I devoured the second burger and egg and glass of rice pudding and caught a subway home.

At Key Food I asked for empty boxes and took away as many as I could carry. I lined them up on my living room floor and put socks and shirts in one, books in another. I had expected to go back to the supermarket for more boxes but saw that in short order everything I owned would be put away and accounted for. It was that simple, to pack up my life. I had always wished to live frugally, to keep encumbrances to a minimum, but I was startled by the compactness of my existence. I began to remove things from the boxes, putting books back into the bookcase, clothing back into the bedroom dresser.

I fell asleep quickly and dreamed of a long black train passing through an empty nighttime countryside. The land was perfectly silent and still, but the train clattered and ground and spewed out vast plumes of black, stringy smoke. The smoke smelled horrible, and I knew that it came from something bad within the shuddering train. Eventually I came to understand that a body was being burned, that someone was trying to conceal a crime. I opened my eyes in the dark. I felt hot. I knew it wasn't morning. There was, in fact, a noxious smell.

There was also noise—a noise as of someone moving about the living room, pushing aside the drapes, dragging a chair across the floor. I put my ear to the door. It was warm, and I knew then what was happening. I knew it would not be a good idea to open the door. I went to the window and looked down to the concrete sidewalk with its one scraggly tree, calculating whether it was too high to jump. There was no phone in the bedroom. I grabbed my wallet and pushed the Tuckerman book under the waistband of my pajamas. Then I went back to the door, dropped to my knees, and opened it slowly.

The flames were swaying and shivering up the window curtains, which gave off a rustling, spitting sound. It was very bright by the windows. A thin line of smoke curled upward from the carpet. I looked left, at my half-emptied bookcases, and then right, toward the kitchen, which was an obscure tapestry of smoke and light. I heard a popping sound, and with astonishing speed a bolt of flame shot across the ceiling.

Keeping my head between my knees, I crawled across the hot carpet, trying not to hurry. The air was thick, alien. Hold on to the breath that's already in you, I told myself, hold on to it until you get to the front door. Don't breathe. But the trip was long and I had to take little sips of air that clogged my throat and burned my lungs. Finally my knee banged up against something hard. I reached up for the knob and then yanked my fingers back—hot. I fumbled my shirt over my head and onto my hand, wrenched the door open. Coolness and darkness now. Gasping, I stumbled down the stairs. The street was completely quiet. I limped, blowing on my seared fingers, until I reached a building that I knew had a doorman. The doorman called 911 and then pulled from his stand, as if they had been waiting just for me, a pair of beat-up leather slippers. I stood with the slippers and shirt in my hand, shivering, until the doorman said gently, looking at my bare feet, "Put those things on now. You must be freezing."

For a long time that evening I sat in a fire truck, a fireman's spare coat spread across my lap, my fingers wrapped in gauze moistened with bacitracin, occasionally glancing up at the windows of my apartment. Once it became clear that the fire would not be put out quickly, once I heard one of the men shout that both the second and third floors were engulfed in flames, I found that I could not stay awake. I pounded my knees to fight off sleep and reminded myself that my home and all my possessions were being destroyed, but drowsiness pulled me under. Later a man stood over me, shaking me alert. His face was blackened and his mustache was caked with ice. "Bad luck," he said. He searched my face and I wondered if he had been here the first time, if he suspected me of something. He told me, gesturing upward, that I couldn't go back inside. Just then a large piece of glass detached itself from a window and fell, spinning in the air before shattering on the pavement. I wondered who would clean up the mess. An image came to me of Mrs. Fiore sweeping the hallways. The fireman asked if I had any money on me, any identification, any place to stay. I said yes to the first two, then no. "You're going to need some help," he told me. He opened a compartment in the door of the truck and pulled out a sheet of paper, a grainy photocopy, pointing out the numbers for the Emergency Assistance Unit, the Department of Homeless Services, the Red Cross. He told me that I might be entitled to free counseling. I sat holding the paper, not understanding. Finally the fireman put a hand on my shoulder. "All right," he said. "It's 3:00 AM. You come back to the station with us."

The truck drove without sirens, gliding like a big boat in the night. In the station there was a smell of sausages, frying eggs. I ate a breakfast, murmured thank-yous. I was shown to an empty cot but could not sleep; it was as if in the truck I had slept for weeks. I forced myself to imagine my furniture igniting, the big oak bookshelves falling off the wall, the books on them crumbling into ash. I could not bring myself to care. It seemed as if I had already lost these things years ago. What it hurt me to think of was the shard of glass from Patrick's shoe, the soiled little note in his handwriting, the photograph. Couldn't I have grabbed these on my way out? I had already forgotten the circumstances under which I'd left, the fear and the crawling. I gazed out the window as the sun came up and the television played in the rec room and men shouting "Gin!" slapped cards upon a table.

Thirteen

Many of the bonsai have died. I have been too brutal; some of the older plants I should have left alone. I should have realized that they could not withstand such drastic alteration. When the bonsai die, they die quickly, their crowns turning brown overnight and their trunks going gray and chalky. But perhaps there was no way to predict, because some of the trees I thought were the most damaged, the least malleable, have survived the ordeal of replanting, their leaves greening and their branches developing swelling nodules that will bear leaves. I am stricken about the others and cannot bring myself to dump them unceremoniously in the same bin where I put the clippings and other debris. Instead I dig a large hole behind the shed and line it with the dead plants, then fill it in with dirt and smooth it over.

On my second Saturday at Endicott's Nursery a customer walks out of the greenhouse toward the shed where I am working, two little girls trailing behind her. I know even before I can fully see them that they are identical twins, five or six years old. They have thin freckled faces and straight red hair and a rangy, underfed look. The woman tells me with some irritation that there's no one in the greenhouses, she needs some salvia.

I wipe my hands on my apron and lead her to the salvia flats. "You know, there isn't enough help around here," the woman says sourly. One of the little girls sidles up to her and leans against her, clutching her pants leg. Her thumb is plugged firmly into her mouth. Her twin inspects the flats, poking her fingers into the dirt. "Stop that," her mother snaps.

The girl continues jabbing the flats and stares at her mother challengingly. "I hate you," she says.

The woman raises her hand to strike, then glances at me and puts her hand down. "What kind of talk is that from a little girl?" she asks. "If I'd ever said that to my own mother she would have tanned my bottom so I wouldn't sit down for a week. Yours too, I bet."

"Shall I ring this up for you?" I ask. The mother walks away holding her plants. The twins fall in step behind her and in unison they stick out their tongues at her back. Then they giggle, mashing their hands against their mouths.

That evening, counting out my cash, Mr. Endicott says he has received some complaints about me since I started working at the nursery. Customers say I am unfriendly, that I make them uneasy. I stand too far away, I don't appear to listen. I don't give helpful answers to their questions. I stare down at my hands while Mr. Endicott speaks. I have lost weight since my arrival at the abbey and the hands look bony to me, naked.

"I will try to do better," I tell him.

Fourteen

The Calliope was once a grand hotel, to judge by the cavernous lobby with its fading mural of unicorns and dancing nymphs and youths being fed from baskets of grapes and berries. The vaulted ceiling was still golden in patches, but there were long brown stains the width of a finger running down the nymphs' faces and pooling dirtily beside the youths' sandaled feet. Whatever it once was, the Calliope was now a transient hotel, charging by the week, where the city's Emergency Assistance Unit referred "burnt-outs," as they called people like me. It was only twenty blocks uptown from my apartment, and I considered it a good omen to have been placed so close to my old neighborhood. The day after the fire, in borrowed clothes, I went to my bank and drew upon my meager savings, then installed myself in a room containing one sink, a hot plate, a refrigerator no taller than my knee, and a clothesline that stretched between the closet and a nail in the wall. I bought two shirts, two pairs of pants, underwear and socks, a coat, and some food. After this burst of activity I sank into a profound fatigue. Despite my hunger—I had not eaten since my middle-of-the-night breakfast at the fire station—I could not rouse myself to make a meal. From the room next door came the tantalizing smell of spices and cooking meat. I'd seen a foreign-looking family of six leave that room earlier in the day, the mother carrying an enormous garbage bag, the four children running zigzags behind her. I wondered how they managed to cook meat on an electric hot plate. I listened to the children's muffled chatter and the laughter and scolding of the grown-ups.

The next morning I awakened having forgotten where I was, and when the room with its four corners and squat refrigerator came back to me I huddled again under the covers. I had dreamed of the baskets of fruit on the mural, of lying in the grass and being fed by long slender hands. Eventually I forced myself upright and arranged my groceries on the counter: cornflakes, white rice, a can of black beans. I could smell the family next door again. Something oatmeal-like this time but more exotic, something warm and grainy and sweet. Disheartened, I left the cornflakes alone and got myself dressed. My hands trembled so badly that it was hard to button the shirt, but nevertheless I disdained the elevator and walked the seven flights down to the lobby. This energized me momentarily. I nodded to the bored guard who sat at the reception desk, and strode out into the bright sun like a man with a plan. But as soon as I reached the sidewalk I felt weak again. I picked my way slowly downtown, scanning the unfamiliar streets for a place to eat. At the first diner I came to all the booths were taken, so I sat on a stool at the front and ordered eggs, French toast, home fries, sausage, and coffee. As soon as the plates appeared in front of me I realized that I had not brought any money. The waitress's eyes narrowed suspiciously as I stuttered out an explanation, but then, studying me further, they softened.

"You come back tomorrow and pay me," she said. "It'll be all right." She winked conspiratorially.

The smell of sausage and browned potatoes rose from the plate; my mouth was wet with need. "No," I said. "I can't pay." I could not bear her standing there feeling pity for me, believing that I had tried to cheat her.

"Don't leave, honey," she said, but I was already on my way.

It was just as well, I thought, as my feet moved me automatically southward, in the direction of my old neighborhood. Eating out was an extravagance. Cereal in my room, inexpensive staples: that was what I ought to be content with. Just when I felt that I must stop and catch my breath, I saw that I was near my old library branch. I went in, glad for the familiar room and for the smell of books and overcoats. I sat at a table and put my head in my arms until someone touched me on the shoulder and told me that no sleeping was allowed in the library. I looked up and recognized one of the librarians.

"Oh, hello," she stammered, flustered. She did not know my name but had often seen me here. "That's all right," I told her. "I'm sorry, I wasn't feeling well." I walked past the circulation desk and onto the street, where I supported myself against an iron railing. When my eyes stopped swimming I saw across the way a traffic island with two benches, one mercifully free, and I crossed over to it and sank down to rest.

The next day, fortified by a quick meal in my room, I went straight to the library and, in an attempt to broadcast health and purpose, walked stiffly erect to the nearest wall of shelves, which happened to hold a set of encyclopedias. I took down the first volume and opened to page one.

> A. The name of this letter in the Phoenician period resembled the Hebrew name *aleph*, meaning "ox"; the form is thought to derive from an early symbol resembling the head of an ox.

> *Aardvark*, "earth-pig," the Afrikaans name for an exclusively African termite-eating mammal of the genus *Orycteropus*, comprising the order Tubulidentata (q.v.). . . .

I read for a few hours, through *Adelaide*, a tenth-century Italian empress, skipping some overlong bits on accounting and Aberdeenshire in Scotland. The librarian who had surprised me the day before passed my table, nodding encouragingly. Sometime after noon I stood up, refreshed, no more certain than I had been that morning of what the future held, but convinced that I would find a way to meet it. *If I come back tomorrow*, I thought, *I'll be able to read as far as* Aeronautics; *the next day will take me through* Africa.

Day by day I felt stronger. One morning, instead of stopping at the library, I kept on walking. There was a spring omen in the air, the scent of hairline cracks in buried seeds. Heartened by the unusually mild weather, I splurged on a loaf of bakery bread, stuffing the ragged chunks into my mouth. Soon, I told myself, I would visit the park. Was the witch-hazel bush thriving? As I walked, I mentally went over my finances. I had enough money in the bank to stay at the Calliope for another four weeks, maybe five. And then what? An office job? Who would hire me, after fifteen years out of work, even to do typing? I tried to picture myself as a supermarket cashier or telemarketer. I tried to imagine repeating the same dull activities over and over again for hours at a stretch, punching numbers into a cash register or repeating a sales pitch to people I called at home during the dinner hour. What about a job in the library? I conjured up the boxy, well-lit room, the pleasant rustle of magazines. I resolved to speak to the librarian, even as it occurred to me that library jobs required advanced degrees and computer skills. Perhaps I could be hired to clean the library?

When I reached the Chelsea Zen Center it was 9:00 AM. I sat on my stoop, chewing the end of my loaf, keeping my eyes on the front door. Today would be the day that Patrick would come; I was sure of it. The hours passed and I waited, expectant, glad. I imagined taking a walk with Patrick in the park, pointing out the plants pressing toward their bloom time, naming them for him. Did he know their names? I touched the book in my coat pocket for reassurance.

Just before one o'clock his tall form rounded the corner and the blood rushed to my head as I spotted his lope, the pants that flapped loose on his legs. That I'd had a premonition of his arrival convinced me that I was graced with some special intuition today, that everything I did from here on would be magical, correct. I waited until Patrick entered the building, then crossed the street and followed him in. His face would light up when he saw me; he would grow nervous, appealingly unsure of himself. *I've been wondering about you since the fire*, he would tell me. *How are you doing? Where did you go?* I would hint that I had found comfortable lodgings, that everything was all right. Then I would hand him the book, saying, *I have been meaning to give you this as a thank-you. For the photograph you brought me.*

But Jack, with all you've been through! Were you able to save anything at all? . . . I'm so sorry. Is there anything I can do?

If it's not too much trouble, perhaps you could bring me another copy of the photograph.

Of course!

In my pocket I would find one of the scrap-paper cards from the library, and on it I would neatly write the phone number of the Calliope.

He would turn the pages of the book.

Frederick Goddard Tuckerman. I've never heard of him.
Thank you. I love poetry.

A pair of white orchids stood in a tall vase on an altar at
the front of the meditation room. Patrick took off his shoes,
and from my spot a few feet away I could see his dark socks
threaded with silver. He sat down on a cushion and tucked
his hair behind his ears, a sweet, childish movement that
made me shiver. I walked forward, my heart in my mouth,
clutching the book of sonnets. But another man cut into
my path, saying Patrick's name, and I shrank back, first in
surprise, then with an instinct to hide. Patrick stood up and
the man put his arm around his shoulder. The man said
something genial, and Patrick put his lips to his cheek. I
sank back against a wall, forcing myself to watch. Patrick's
hand dropped low on the man's back and rested there as if
this were the most natural thing in the world, as if this spot
and his hand were old companions.

The bell sounded for the meditation session to begin.
Patrick sat down and the man stepped back. Trapped, I sat
down, too, stuffing the book back into my pocket. Were
Patrick and the man lovers? I focused my eyes on the sun-
struck floor and listened to the sounds of breathing, the
rustlings of people still arranging themselves on their mats.
The book poked into my thigh, making it impossible to get
comfortable. I followed the sound of footsteps: someone
was walking slowly up and down the aisles. It must have
been the man who opened and closed the doors, the one in

robes who carried a long painted stick. The leader chanted a brief prayer. Then there was silence.

Were they lovers? I raised my head and looked around, finally spotting Patrick in the row of bodies toward the front. His friend was in the row behind him. I stared at the man's thick curls, his broad neck. When he'd embraced Patrick I'd noted the nylon athletic shirt he was wearing, tight across his chest. The robed monitor caught my eye and frowned. I bent my head and tried to follow my own breathing. If I were to get up and walk four steps forward, I would be standing right next to Patrick. If I called out in a soft voice, he would hear me. I shifted on my mat, shaking some of the ache out of my legs and buttocks. I was turning my gaze back to Patrick, past the gold Buddha grinning on the altar, when I heard a loud crack and a fiery pain spread across my shoulders. My head snapped back in alarm, my heart pounded. The monitor was already on his way down the aisle, calmly holding the stick with which he had struck me. A humiliated flush rose to my face. Just then the bell pealed briefly, and another droning chant was intoned. The room filled with the sound of knees cracking, feet testing the floor. I massaged my throbbing shoulder and stood up unsteadily. Patrick, passing by, turned his head with a startled look. Then he was past me and out the door.

A man's hand descended upon my arm. It was the monitor. Up close, he had a round, whiskery face and was a full head shorter than I was. "I hope you don't mind. It's our way here. It's not meant as punishment but to encourage concentration."

"Yes, yes." I was anxious for him to remove his hand, which made it impossible for me to think of anything else.

"I hope you'll return, you're a new face."

"Yes," I said. I grabbed my coat from the floor and hurried away.

Perhaps Patrick would be waiting out front for me, I thought, but the sidewalk was empty. I looked up and down the block, hoping for a glimpse of him. It came to me clearly that if I pretended there was nothing unusual in my having been at the center today then he would not believe that there was. *What a coincidence,* I would say. *And by the way, I have something I've been meaning to give you.*

I headed toward Patrick's office, wondering if I could catch up with him, but as I drew close to the building I lost courage. I changed direction and walked until I saw a restaurant. The young woman at the hostess's stand asked, "Lunch?" and I told her I only wanted to borrow a phone book. There were three Allegras in the Manhattan white pages. The name looked so powerfully beautiful, shining out from the long columns of tiny type, that for a moment I grew dizzy. There was an Allegra, P, on Thirty-Seventh Street. I took down the number and left.

The weather was really fine now: sunny and soft, with a light breeze. Despite the expense I rode the subway uptown, feeling celebratory. The park was busy with bicyclists, joggers, and children. I moved slowly along the paths, feeling as if I had been away for a very long time. The trees swayed, testing the atmosphere, readying themselves for the effort ahead. I entered the Ramble and searched for the witch-hazel bush. When I saw it standing sturdy and healthy among the other bushes I patted it all over in a kind of happy daze. Without admitting to myself what I was doing, I moved gradually in the direction of a well-known spot, a place off the trail that was sheltered by tall Japanese knotweed and marked by a deeply ridged cork tree. When I found the tree I backed myself up against it and waited. Within moments I heard movement in the weeds a couple of yards away. I inched myself a quarter circle around the tree, listened again. There was panting now, and, in counterpoint, a low rhythmic whimpering. I wished that I could see the men, the position of their legs and arms and heads, the contortions of their faces. I imagined a two-tiered creature with four arms, four legs, two heads: something fearsome and fascinating at the same time. All at once there was a gurgling sound and then a jagged explosion of breath, like someone expressing impatience. I pressed myself against the tree, aware of how exposed I was, aware that if either of the men exited in my direction they would see me in my spy's crouch. My heart was loud in my ears as first one and then another set of footsteps moved in the opposite direction. I stood up, bathed in sweat, and restored my equilibrium by carefully folding my coat over my arm, like a man about to leave an office meeting. I combed my hand through my hair. Then I moved with shaky steps back onto the trail. A middle-aged woman with thick hips and bird-watcher's binoculars on a beaded chain around her neck studied me sternly as I emerged.

I walked until I was steadier again and could trust myself to sit quietly. Then I found a bench and closed my eyes, listening to the footfalls and fragments of conversation that passed me by. I pictured my face as if from above, my eyelids translucent in the sunlight, veins visible in my forehead, the age lines around my mouth etched in place.

"Watch out, Dylan!" came a shout close by, and I looked out into the world to find a boy in a heap on top of my outstretched feet. His mother bent over him, her perfume flooding my nostrils, and asked if he was hurt. But it became clear that the cause of the boy's tears was the empty ice-cream cone he was holding up to her view like a snuffed torch. The ice cream had landed on my pants. I shook it off as best I could, but a sticky cold had already begun to seep through the cheap fabric.

The woman lifted the boy to his feet and apologized to me. "I'm so sorry. Of course I'll pay for the dry cleaning."

A rivulet of ice cream ran down the leg of my pants as I stood up and reached into my pocket. The Tuckerman book was wet, the cover tacky when I pressed it with my finger. I shook my head at the woman and began to jog toward Central Park West.

Back at the hotel I tore off the pants and filled the sink with soapy water. I dabbed the book with a wet washcloth, which only seemed to make the stain spread. Anxiously I blotted it, then put it on the windowsill to dry. Then I dressed in my other pair of pants and walked down the hall to the pay phone.

It was not yet evening. Patrick would not be home; he need never know that I had called. Would there be an answering machine? Would someone else pick up—perhaps the man from the meditation hall? After three rings, a machine clicked on, and Patrick's voice spoke melodiously into my ear: "I'm sorry I've missed you. I'd like to talk to you, so please leave a message." I knew these words were not meant especially for me, and yet it seemed to me that they were, that it could not be entirely arbitrary that I was hearing them now. I hung up, dug in my pocket for another quarter, and dialed again. "I'd like to talk to you." After this I resisted the temptation to call again and reluctantly went back to my room to spend the evening reading a book the librarian had given me. She had come up to my carrel the previous afternoon. "I wondered if you might enjoy this," she said. "We just got it in." She glanced down at the encyclopedia as if its contents now worried her. Then she put the book, a murder mystery, next to it and walked away without saying anything more. I didn't look at it until I got home. The opening disgusted me, a description of a woman stabbed and left for dead in an alleyway. Yet I read on, looking over my shoulder every so often as if someone were watching me and might disapprove.

I slept that night even more poorly than usual. The hotel at night was never quiet; at all hours I woke to the banging of doors, music, sobbing, arguments. Every day I told myself that soon I would get used to it all, that one morning my body would feel the simple refreshment of a good night's rest. But the days had passed and I had not gotten used to the noises; on the contrary, they had begun to inflame me more and more, so that even quiet footsteps in the hallway or a neighbor's soft snoring made my eyes fly wide open. That night the book the librarian gave me entered my dreams with images of blood and death and caused me to wake, shouting silently. Finally I got up and ate my breakfast sleepily, watching the time. Did Patrick get to work at nine? At ten? It did not seem to me that I could wait that long to call again and hear his voice telling me he wanted to speak to me. At eight-thirty I hurried down the corridor and dropped a coin into the phone. Surely he would have left by now. I listened anxiously to one ring, then another, then relaxed as the third ring heralded the click of the answering machine. It was only as I heard the same words again that I realized how sorry I was that he had not answered in person.

The rest of the day was oppressively long. I walked down to the West Twenties, pushing myself on with impatient words whenever I was tired and tempted to stop. This walk would have been nothing to me in the old days, I reminded myself. But I was exhausted by the time I drew near Patrick's office. I dared not approach the building too closely. I did not want to surprise him again. I re-created the look he had given me in the meditation room and tried to read into it some sign of pleasure or welcome. On a stoop some blocks away I ground the heels of my hands into my sore eyes. Then I thought about the journey home and tears leaked from under my hands. I was simply too tired to walk back. I removed a precious bill and two quarters from my wallet, then limped over to the subway.

At five-thirty that evening I began to call Patrick. I called every fifteen minutes, strictly waiting out the time interval, watching as each coin disappeared down the slot forever. Once I hung up just as the machine clicked on, in the hope that my coin would be returned to me, but the trick didn't work, and I was only cheated of the sound of Patrick's voice. At six-thirty I began to get upset. Hadn't I waited a good long time already? Shouldn't Patrick be home by now? I began to call every ten minutes, then every five. By seven-forty, when Patrick picked up the phone, my throat was so swollen with disappointment that at first I could not speak a word.

"Hello?" Patrick said. And then again: "Hello?"

"Patrick, Patrick, it's Jack Ronan. Jack Gorse. Good God, I don't know who I am anymore." I laughed and before he could reply I began hurriedly to explain why I had been at the Zen center the previous day, babbling something about my lifelong interest in Buddhism, realizing that with each word I piled on it became more and more obvious that I had been there solely to see him, that our meeting had not been an accident. I scratched at my neck, hot with discomfort. Patrick tried to get a word in, but I could not stop myself. I repeated something or other I had read about the differences between Japanese and Korean Buddhism. Finally a sentence got through to me. "Where are you calling from?" he asked, and it came back to me, the long, dim hallway smelling of beans and stale coffee, the musty carpeting, room after room filled with people who had lost their homes.

"I'm at a hotel," I said. "For the meanwhile."

"I was wondering what had happened to you. Have you been all right?"

The words I had imagined, the very words. I flushed with pleasure and clutched the receiver more tightly.

"Yes," I said. "I'm good. I'm really good."

There was a brief silence on the other end. "Do you need money?"

"No," I answered, shocked. I tried to purge my voice of any need or trouble. "It's the photograph. You know, the one you took of me." I poured out my explanation: I missed the picture, couldn't get it out of my mind. It was a beautiful piece, really a work of art. Might he have another copy?

I sank down into a crouch, stretching the phone cord taut, and closed my eyes.

"I'm flattered," Patrick said slowly. "But I don't have one just now. I could print up another copy, of course. It might take me a few days."

I assured him there was no hurry.

"Well, all right, then. Just tell me where to send it."

"Actually," I said, pushing the receiver hard against my collarbone to keep from shaking, "would you mind meeting in person?" The hotel wasn't very good with mail, I explained. They'd lost something from my bank just the other day. I said that the best place to meet would be the old apartment. My hotel was very far uptown. Besides, I had yet to go over there to inspect. I still intended to salvage anything that might be salvageable.

He hesitated, but something told me that if I calmly pressed the point he would do what I wanted. "There's no rush," I insisted again. "Whenever it's convenient for you."

"Just a sec." There was a rustling and then he asked me if I was free the following Thursday at six. He could stop by, he said, after a meeting with a client.

I said that Thursday at six would be fine.

As soon as I hung up the phone I began to laugh. I was going to see Patrick. I had no place to live, no job, almost no money, but I was going to see Patrick. I walked back to my room and stretched out on my bed. To see him again, feel his presence, speak a few words—that was all I wanted. I was not greedy. And maybe something I would say or do would make him feel that he did not want this to be our last meeting.

The ceiling, I noted, had a long brown crack in the shape of a question mark. This made me laugh again. Even question marks appeared to be in my favor; whatever was to happen was sure to be right and good. There were six days until I would see Patrick—six days. How would I fill them? I retrieved the Tuckerman book from the windowsill and leafed through the familiar sonnets. The stain on the cover had not vanished completely when it had dried and it now looked like a large ghostly thumbprint. I could not keep my mind on the words.

That night, for the first time since I could remember, I slept deeply and well. I woke early, alert and hungry, and after a quick breakfast I left the hotel and walked to Central Park. I passed through Mariners' Gate in the dawn chill, filling my lungs with the smell of thawed earth and old rocks and pollen. Spring was coming in a rush. The crocuses and daffodils were out in full strength, forsythia was swelling on the branch, ready to burst forth. Within days the magnolia would push out its spoon-shaped petals. The early red maples were in leaf and glittering in the sun. Most years I had mixed emotions about the coming of spring, the simultaneous arrival of bloom and busyness: all the bodies, noise, and music that filled the park in fair weather. The runners and in-line skaters and jugglers and mimes, the political pamphleteers, horseback riders, martial-arts practitioners: all of these crowded me deeper into the Ramble, into the uninhabited gaps in the park. But today I was only grateful, feeling as if this spring was one I might easily have been deprived of. I was alive, I was here to see it. I fell in with a group taking a nature walk and listened as an elderly woman in an army surplus jacket and Yankees cap pointed out plants and early-spring birds. I enjoyed pretending to know nothing, to be as blank as the woman who asked if a spruce was a pine. "Look," said the tour guide, indicating a squirrel with a bitten-off ear and empty eye socket. "Winter's hard on everyone."

Afterward I walked to Egret, stood by the front desk, and waited as the tinny sound of the bells subsided. Finally Carl could not resist raising his head. "I've been sick," I told him. "Sorry to hear that," he replied gruffly, and returned to his papers. I smiled and went to explore the stacks. But when I arrived at the Stardust Marion refused to look at me. She stared into the distance as she waited for my order, tapping her pencil on her pad as if ticking off demerits for disloyalty, abandonment. I pretended not to notice. The next day I came back and it was the same. By the third day she had forgiven me. She slid a plate of home fries next to my coffee, telling me that the kitchen had sent it out by accident. "It'll just go in the garbage otherwise," she said.

In the evenings I went to the library. I would have liked instead to walk to the water as I used to, to climb the Brooklyn Bridge as the sun set. But I knew I did not have the strength.

Ambrose, Saint (340?–397), bishop of Milan, one
of the great doctors of the Western church, born in
Trier of a Roman senatorial family.

Every day or two the librarian came by with a new book for me. She had grown more talkative and sometimes told me why she was recommending it. She had seen a glowing review of this one in the librarians' journal, or she had read the book and couldn't put it down. She loved murder mysteries. I took whatever she gave me, but the murder tales I didn't read. I needed no more nightmares. The other books I did plow through, even when they didn't interest me. The librarian looked at me so eagerly when she came bearing her gifts that I felt obliged to try. So I dutifully read a collection of humor pieces by a television comedian and a first novel by a young immigrant writer, and forgot them as soon as I was done.

On Thursday evening I arrived at my old building long before it was necessary. I had thought of a thousand different ways our meeting might go, had daydreamed of conversations that ended with a smile or a touch, with our walking away from the building together or going our separate ways. For the first time it occurred to me that Patrick might not come at all. Perhaps he would forget, perhaps he had never intended to come. From a dozen yards away I could see the scaffolding and orange plastic netting that covered the brownstone from top to bottom. Wooden boards covered the windows. I ducked under a platform and stood at the top of my old stoop, rubbing the soot-streaked stone.

When Patrick arrived, at ten after six, I hoped I looked presentable. I emerged from my little alcove, waving, slapping grime off my coat and hands. Patrick slouched, gestured upward at the damaged building with his chin. "There it is," he said. "The shell of a beautiful place." The sight clearly depressed him. Then, unexpectedly, he threw his arms around me and hugged me. He pounded me gently on the back. "How are you getting along?" he asked.

My head was jammed against his shoulder and I did not know what to do with my arms, which were pinned against my sides. All I could sense was the sharpness of Patrick's collarbone and the vaguely musty scent of his neck and the thick sausage feel of my trapped arms.

He let go, waited for an answer.

"Let's go in," I said. I felt as if I were about to weep. I blinked, trying to keep hold of myself.

"I hope you're prepared. Nothing has been cleaned up yet." He took a key from his pocket and unlocked a large padlock securing the outer door.

It was dim inside; the overhead light had been smashed. The walls were pocked and smeared with ashy streaks, the stairs were filthy. I stepped around broken glass, bits of metal. Patrick urged me to walk slowly, pointed out areas on the landing where the floor was spongy or the support beams showed through. "Careful, careful," he repeated. I could feel him behind me, very close, his solicitousness, his anxious hovering. For a moment I saw myself as Mrs. Fiore, an old woman helped up the stairs by a kind young man. The door to my apartment stood open, partially off its hinges. The first thing I realized was that part of the floor inside had fallen into the apartment below, and part of Mrs. Fiore's floor had fallen into mine. The resulting chaos made it hard to tell what anything was. There were odd bits of fabric, hunks of metal and glass, broken Sheetrock, burnt pieces of wood, gray ash, black ash, twisted pieces of what looked like plastic. Close to the center of the room squatted a monstrous blackened conch—the coffee table, I eventually determined, buckled inward by the heat. A scrap of drapery drooped from a boarded window like a flag of surrender.

Patrick remained silent as I checked my bedroom, where a burned mattress lay with exposed springs. It gave off such a powerful stench that I gagged. A piece of paper blew back and forth in the draft from a broken window. I picked it up, thinking it might be a page from a book, something I might recognize, but it was a fragment of a restaurant delivery menu.

"Why don't we go around the corner for a cup of coffee," Patrick suggested. "We'll sit a minute."

"No, I want to stay here."

I tried to take in all that I was seeing. I had thought that I would be moved, maybe that I would cry, but I could not seem to wring anything out of myself. I scooped up a handful of ashes, let it trickle from my fingers. Irritably, I asked: "Do you have the photograph?"

Patrick took off his knapsack and handed the envelope to me. I opened it and was again caught off guard by that bewildered, unready expression, that look of bracing against a possible blow. Over the weeks I had touched up the image in memory, smoothed the hair, put light and focus into the eyes. Now I was again disheartened by the portrait, vaguely insulted even.

"Why did you take my picture?" I asked.

Patrick took the photograph from my hands, studied it. "You didn't have a social face," he said. "Often when I'm taking pictures I get impatient at the social faces. People want to look sexy or smart or strong or whatever. They want to be in control of the look. I'm always trying to get underneath that. But you just stood there as if no one had taken your photograph before. You had no look, but I couldn't decide *what* you had."

The ash in my hands was oily, left a coating even when I scuffed my palms against each other. "You take people's pictures all the time," I said. The thought struck me unpleasantly.

He heard the complaint in my voice and looked at me in surprise. "I've been working on this project," he said. "I document people like you, people who are getting pushed out of their apartments. Mostly in Manhattan, sometimes in other places."

People like you. I took this in for a moment. Then I asked, "Whatever for?"

Well, Patrick explained, he loved what he did. He loved building things, creating spaces for people to live and work in. But after a while it had become hard to look away from the human cost, from the people who were being forced to leave and change their lives because a building was being renovated or torn down. When the economy started to boom it was even worse. "There were all these people that the boom had passed by and who knew where they were going to go? When I was meditating I would have flashes of the tenants I had met, even of people's stuff—this one's coatrack, that one's kitchen linoleum. I was bothered by it all."

I sensed that he had told this story before, that it was something he used to explain to other people who he was.

He'd spoken to the abbot about it, he said. The abbot had asked him if he was prepared to give up his work. He said no, he thought there was more good than bad in it. The abbot told him that then he must find a way to bear witness.

"Did you take Mrs. Fiore's picture?" I asked.

"Yes," he said. "She is very beautiful, did you ever notice?"

I asked him what he did with all these pictures.

He smiled. "Actually, I hope one day I'll have a book, or a show, or something. I'd like to think they're good work."

Good work? I turned away, busied myself pushing the photograph back into its envelope. It would not enter easily and I shoved it harder, crushing the edges. Instantly I felt a prick of remorse.

"I didn't mean to upset you," Patrick said. "Hurting you is the last thing I want to do. I should have said something, maybe. Look, if you dislike the photo I'll destroy it."

"Yes, destroy it," I told him.

He looked unhappy at that. "Do me one favor," he said. "Don't decide that just now, when you're upset. Think about it and get back to me, and I promise to do whatever you want. But I feel like I need to tell you it's the best portrait I've ever done. I find it impossible to take a good picture of someone unless I care about them in some way."

I clutched the envelope in both hands and forced myself to meet his eyes. It seemed to me that meeting his eyes was the important thing, that it would tell me the truth of what he felt and maybe even of what I felt. I looked in his eyes and he held my gaze. My heart rose up in my chest and knocked wildly. The pause lengthened, became awkward. I must say something, do something. The moment was slipping away.

"I love you," I said.

Patrick's eyes widened and in the flicker of embarrassment that ran through them I read everything I needed to know. Apparently *I care about you* did not mean the same thing as *I love you*. I stared at my feet, mortified.

"Jack—"

The note of compassion in his voice was unbearable. I could see the photograph before me, painfully vivid, on a book page with a caption running beneath: *Jack Gorse, 40, Upper West Side. Evicted from his one-bedroom apartment after fifteen years. When his funds ran out after a stint in a transient hotel . . .*

I put my hand on the mantelpiece to steady myself, felt the powdery grit beneath it. I lifted it and stared at my sooty palm.

"Listen, Jack."

I picked up the poker leaning against the fireplace. It felt pliable in my hands, as if still soft from the heat that had ignited the room. I held it up as I walked toward him.

"Tell me that you love me," I said.

He looked at me in disbelief, took a step backward.

"I don't even care if it's not true. Just tell me that you love me," I insisted.

"Jack, I . . ."

"Tell me!"

I moved toward him, wagging the poker slowly to and fro. All the time I was thinking, *You can't hit him. You won't. You wouldn't do such a thing.*

His mouth was working, and he said, in a thin, rushed voice, "I love you."

"No, you don't mean it," I told him. "I want you to really mean it. Please try to mean it."

I told myself I would not hurt him if he would just try, that I would not hurt him in any event, but that for just a few more moments I needed to keep him here and force him to talk to me, force him to consider the idea—just consider it—of loving me.

Then he did something I did not expect. He stopped backing up and his face cleared. He looked at me with great sadness and said, softly but very distinctly, "I hardly know you."

Then I hit him. I raised my arm and swung the poker against the side of his head. Later I told myself that I had checked myself at the last moment, that I had not hit him with all my might. Was that true? His knees bent and he fell hard to one side, and I thought of the sack of groceries that Mrs. Fiore had dropped on the landing, the way the cans of vegetables had rumbled into the corner. I still half believed, as I put my hand to Patrick's cheek, that I had not hit him, that I would never actually hit another human being. He was breathing, his cheek moved shallowly under my palm, but his eyes were closed, his mouth gently parted like a child's. Blood was trickling out of his ear. I dropped the poker and ran through the open door, down the stairs. I stood in front of the blighted building turning this way and that, not knowing where to go. For a moment I thought of going back upstairs to tend to him but if I went back I would have to ask him again if he loved me, and I could not bear to think of that. In the end, habit served me. I crossed the avenue and fled through Mariners' Gate, toward the Ramble.

Fifteen

Somehow I thought not to run. There was no reason to run. What I had done had been justified, unavoidable. I moved past the bench sitters and nuzzling couples into the more thinly populated interior of the park, and when I found myself in a stretch of the Ramble with no one in sight I walked into a stand of Japanese knotweed until I reached a spot where the plants grew higher than my head. Then I curled into the cold earth. I touched my hands in the waning light, feeling for the telltale wetness of blood, and thought of prison, of being led out of a courtroom with my hands shackled, in leg irons. I thought of lights blazing at all hours in a concrete cell, of being forced to march in a line, of guards who took pleasure in making me uncomfortable and afraid. I told myself quite reasonably that I could never survive in such a place, that I would have to find a way to kill myself first.

I dozed off. I woke to complete darkness and the sound
of rain. After a moment I discovered it was not rain but
someone relieving himself in the knotweed. I wanted to tell
him to go home, that it was not safe here at this hour. After
the man passed into the distance, I fell asleep once more.
In the morning there was the hollow rattling of a wood-
pecker, the sound of mockingbirds. Instinctively I patted
my pocket; my wallet was still there but the book for Patrick
was not. I scrabbled about with my hands but could not
find it anywhere.

I stood up, my clothing damp from the morning mist,
raked my hair back from my head, rubbed my face with the
heel of my hand. It was very early and I saw no one about.
I walked through the park toward my hotel, stopping at the
coffee shop where a few weeks earlier the waitress had offered to give me a meal. I sat again at the counter, trying to
catch her eye, and when she came to take my order I os-
tentatiously laid my wallet next to my napkin and ordered
what I had ordered that first time: sausage and eggs, French
toast and home fries and coffee. I could tell that the waitress
did not remember me, but that did not matter. I had successfully passed for someone unexceptional, someone who
simply needed to eat breakfast before going on with his day.
I ate slowly, for I still had time to waste, and I left a siz-
able tip, thinking of Marion. When I reached the Calliope it
was only seven-thirty. I asked the desk guard if anyone had
been to see me since the previous evening. He checked the
overnight guard's report sheet and my pigeonhole and said,

"Sorry, no." I went upstairs and walked directly down the hall to the pay phone.

A voice answered, thick and disoriented, with sleep or perhaps something else. "Hello?" Patrick said. "Who is this?"

I hung up quietly and then put my clothes and some food into a shopping bag. I wrote a letter to the management company for the Calliope Hotel, explaining that I would be vacating my room as of the end of the week. Then I began to walk toward the Port Authority. On the way I returned the book the librarian had given me the day before; I did not like to let books go overdue. At the station I figured out which bus I needed and boarded it around ten. As I sat watching Westchester and then Danbury and Hartford pass by the window a prickly itch began in my chest and spread up my neck and down my arms until I had to sit on my hands to keep from clawing at myself. Just before dusk I knocked on the great oak door of Infinite Light Abbey and as in a dream or fairy tale I was given entry.

Now the first hints of summer have arrived. I saw forsythia along the West Drive of the park during the last days I spent in Manhattan, and weeks later I saw it again in sprays about the abbey, a second coming. The forsythia is spent now, but there are lilacs, azaleas, geraniums, Japanese wisteria. The beans in the garden begin their long climb. Today it is sunny and I move the remaining bonsai, eleven of them, against the shed windows where they can soak up the warm rays. These are the survivors, the ones that may live fifty, a hundred, two hundred more years.

Joku enters and at first I think he is coming to chat with me and check on the plants. I reflexively tense against the certainty of his loose sleeve catching a branch, his sandals tracking dirt along the floor. He always brings with him a certain amount of disorder. But as soon as I see his face I have a premonition of something different. He looks stricken and anxious, and he hovers near the door as if to make sure he can leave quickly if necessary. After him enters another man, then two at once, standing close to each other. One of the pair is short and has a mustache. The other is a little taller. The man in front is large and thick, with sand-colored hair that creeps down past his ears.

"These men are from the county sheriff's department," says Joku. "They've asked to speak with you."

The sandy-haired man steps toward me. He says his name, but I don't hear it, a whirring noise comes up in my head and drowns it out. I want to tell them that I will come with them, I will cooperate, but that they must not touch me. I smell the man's odor—sweat, cigarettes—as he comes close. He puts his hand on my shoulder. It is not a grip, nothing with force in it, but I have to clench myself all over to keep from pulling away. I do not want to upset anyone. I put down the ball of twine I am holding and let the man lead me through the door.

Joku walks alongside us. "When will he be back? Will we be able to contact him by phone?"

"This may only take a couple of hours," says the man non-committally. The two other men follow a few steps behind. We have moved down the hill, toward the parking lot. A few startled residents who have noticed the police car are standing around watching our progress. I spread my free hand uselessly over my face. One of the men behind me steps forward now to open the rear door of the car and the sandy-haired man guides me in and seats himself to my right. The door closes. The sandy-haired man turns toward me. "You have the right to legal counsel. We'll go over all that when we get to the station." We have pulled out of the driveway now, are navigating the winding roads that lead down from the hill the abbey perches upon into the valley below.

"It doesn't matter," I say.

The man to the left of me turns his head and shoots a look across at his partner. The sandy-haired man remains impassive. "You waive the right to an attorney?" he asks evenly.

"Will I get to see him?" I ask.

The man's eyes narrow. "See who?"

"Patrick. Will he be brought in to see me, to identify me? If I'm charged with anything, will he appear in the court-room?"

"Wait a second," the man says. He fishes around in his back pocket, brings out a flattened notepad. He takes a pen from his jacket, flips to a free page in the notebook, writes something down. Then he says, looking over the pad of paper, "I can't say."

"Is it likely?" I ask. "That's all I want to know. What are the chances?"

The man studies me. He begins to understand. "You want to see him again."

I start to cry. The man turns and stares ahead, waiting for this to pass. I heave deep, shuddering sobs, wanting it to pass too.

"Tell me what I need to do to meet with him," I say, when it's over.

"You can begin by telling me how it all happened," the man says.

Acknowledgements

Thanks to Maddy Tarnofsky, tenants' rights attorney, who gave generously of her time to help me understand the intricacies of New York City landlord-tenant law. Susan Sugar, Karen Baicker, George Diggle, and Robert Levy provided supplementary information and in some cases dug up helpful documents. John Wender and Doug Reeves answered questions about, respectively, architecture and tax law.

Cindi Leive read an early incarnation of this book and Michael Lowenthal a later one. Each offered excellent advice and invaluable encouragement. Elena Sigman cannot possibly guess how much her support and deep understanding buoyed me during the revision process. Robert Robin was a sounding board at a critical juncture. The gang at the Writers Studio regularly fed the waters of inspiration.

On the home front, caregivers Tara Lissade and Kathy Melillo provided me with the time, and the peace of mind, that enabled me to complete this novel. It made all the difference to know that the children were in wonderful hands.

My editor, Jin Soo Kang, was a writer's dream: patient, accessible, frighteningly insightful, always putting the good of the manuscript above everything else.

Anna Stein and Tin House Books (Tony Perez, Nanci McCloskey, et al.) brought *The Understory* a new chance in this beautiful new edition.

Finally, to Jonathan, Abraham, and Hannah: my profoundest love and gratitude, always, for giving me a life beyond the page.

The Understory was a finalist for both the 2007 Los Angeles Times Book Prize for First Fiction and the William Saroyan International Prize for Writing. Pamela Erens's widely acclaimed second novel, *The Virgins*, was a *New York Times* and *Chicago Tribune* Editors' Choice. For many years Erens worked as a magazine editor, including at *Glamour*. She lives in Maplewood, New Jersey.